DODGING LEAD

Clint reacted instinctively, pointing his Colt like his finger and squeezing the trigger. The modified pistol sent a single round through the air, drilling the bandit squarely between the eyes as the other man's gun went off.

A round hissed through the air to Clint's left, scraping along his side, but not leaving much more than a nasty scratch in its wake. The man who fired it, on the other hand, slumped backward and spilled the contents of his head onto the floor.

"Clint, look out!"

It was Willa who'd shouted the warning, and by the time Clint responded, he saw another bandit taking aim at him with a shotgun. . . .

DON'T MISS THESE ALL-ACTION WESTERN SERIES FROM THE BERKLEY PUBLISHING GROUP

THE GUNSMITH by J. R. Roberts

Clint Adams was a legend among lawmen, outlaws, and ladies. They called him . . . the Gunsmith.

LONGARM by Tabor Evans

The popular long-running series about Deputy U.S. Marshal Long—his life, his loves, his fight for justice.

SLOCUM by Jake Logan

Today's longest-running action Western. John Slocum rides a deadly trail of hot blood and cold steel.

BUSHWHACKERS by B. J. Lanagan

An action-packed series by the creators of Longarm! The rousing adventures of the most brutal gang of cutthroats ever assembled—Quantrill's Raiders.

DIAMONDBACK by Guy Brewer

Dex Yancey is Diamondback, a Southern gentleman turned con man when his brother cheats him out of the family fortune. Ladies love him. Gamblers hate him. But nobody pulls one over on Dex . . .

WILDGUN by Jack Hanson

The blazing adventures of mountain man Will Barlow—from the creators of Longarm!

TEXAS TRACKER by Tom Calhoun

Meet J. T. Law: the most relentless—and dangerous—manhunter in all Texas. Where sheriffs and posses fail, he's the best man to bring in the most vicious outlaws—for a price.

J. R. ROBERTS

JOVE BOOKS, NEW YORK

JUST REWARD

A Jove Book / published by arrangement with
the author

PRINTING HISTORY
Jove edition / April 2003

For information address: The Berkley Publishing Group,
a division of Penguin Putnam Inc.,
375 Hudson Street, New York, New York 10014.

ISBN: 0-515-13514-3

A JOVE BOOK®
Jove Books are published by The Berkley Publishing Group,
a division of Penguin Putnam Inc.,
375 Hudson Street, New York, New York 10014.
JOVE and the "J" design
are trademarks belonging to Penguin Putnam Inc.

PRINTED IN THE UNITED STATES OF AMERICA

10 9 8 7 6 5 4 3 2 1

ONE

It had been a long ride. From one end of the country to the other, he'd made his mark the only way he knew how: in blood.

Kevin Stohls leaned back in his saddle and took a moment to look back at his life. He didn't have much time to indulge in nostalgia, but he did manage to put a smile on his face when he thought back to all the proud moments of his life.

Not many men could say they had no regrets. Sure, most men *said* that, but they were full of shit. Most men said that just so they wouldn't be too unhappy with the life they'd made for themselves, which seemed to be more of a trench that got deeper and deeper with every passing year.

Men said they liked their families and enjoyed spending their lives in the town where they were born, but the simple truth was that they simply didn't have any other choice. They were stuck, and the best they could think to do about it was to try and convince themselves that they were right where they wanted to be.

After all, words were a hell of a lot cheaper than anything that required a person to get up off his lazy ass and do something. Dreams were even cheaper, but they hit a man like a solid shot below the belt. And since most men didn't have the gumption to take a swing at their dreams, they stood around in bars and blustered about how great they had it.

Stohls stood around in bars a lot, too. He savored the heat of cheap whiskey burning his throat and the punch of liquor in his belly. He stood there listening to other men bluster about their wives and children and land and whatever else they'd managed to scrape together. But Stohls heard the truth behind all of that hot wind spewing out of those mouths. He heard the truth.

He recognized the truth because he'd been one of those men himself for a time. It wasn't a very long time, but it had had enough of an impact on him that it changed the rest of his life. Stohls once had a wife who was swollen with his firstborn. He'd had a small farm in Missouri and a few friends in the town nearby who'd known him since he was in short pants.

By all accounts, he'd had a fairly decent life. Standing at the end of the bar in the local saloon, taking up the space that he'd been in so many times that his feet had worn prints into the floor, Stohls found himself going on and on about how good he had it.

He loved his wife.

He loved the simple existence of a farmer.

And he didn't miss the thrills of his youth. Not one bit.

The more he drank, the more Kevin Stohls had realized one thing in particular: All of what he'd been telling himself had been a lie.

Sure, it felt good to say it. Words like that had a special kind of comfort because they made a man feel good about giving up and tossing his lot in with the rest of the sheep. Once he was in the flock, all he had to do was kick back and follow the rest without a care or an individual thought in the world.

That night, standing on the verge of a safe, prosperous life, Kevin Stohls realized that he was one step away from the point of no return. If he stayed there and got himself too wrapped up in his safe little life, he'd be in too deep to claw his way out. The herd would sweep him away until he was planted in the field outside of town right next to all the other farmers and husbands.

Maybe it had been the whiskey affecting his mind. Firewater had a way of making things look more extreme than they really were. But distorted or not, those things that Stohls saw were like a cold hand slapping the drunkenness right out of him. Even after all those years had passed, Stohls could still feel that sobering touch as strongly as he had that night long ago.

He was full of shit.

Stohls knew that at that very moment, standing in his usual spot inside the saloon where everybody knew his name. Talking about how great his life was going to be and how nice it was going to feel to grow old with his woman and raise a herd of his own. That was all a lie. And no matter how comforting it was, Kevin Stohls wasn't about to pledge his life to a lie.

What he'd really wanted was to go back to the way he was before he'd met that woman he'd married. When he was younger, Stohls would disappear with his cousins for weeks at a time, riding and drinking and fighting until they somehow managed to drag themselves home.

That was the life he'd wanted to devote himself to. And when he thought about it, Stohls knew that was the truth. He wasn't much of a churchgoing man, but he would have sworn to the Lord above that he wanted nothing more than to return to the life he was about to leave behind.

Thinking back to that fateful night, Stohls grinned as

he remembered how he'd excused himself from the saloon and gone back to his home. Once there, he made love to his newlywed bride, strapped on his guns, and kissed her good-bye.

She'd looked at him with wide, trusting eyes, knowing for certain that they would be starting their new life together the next day, after a hearty breakfast.

Once Stohls walked out of his new house, he never went back. As for his bride, he had to take a moment of hard concentration to remember her name. He never did forget the look on her face when she'd last seen him. It was full of trust and hope . . . two things that Kevin Stohls never did think were worth much.

He never looked back after that night. He'd been with enough other women to erase her face clean off his memory, like chalk from a board. He didn't know what became of the baby. What he could remember clear as day was the feel of those guns hanging at his side. Those two .44s gave him the only sense of security that could be trusted.

He remembered leaving that new house along with his new family. He remembered walking back into that familiar saloon with his two .44s. And he would never forget the words that came from his mouth when he stepped through those familiar doors.

"Everyone throw your money and valuables on the floor. This is a holdup!"

TWO

A fine day, indeed.

The air was hot, but the wind was cool as it brushed over the sweat on Clint's brow. The ocean was miles away, but he could smell the hint of salt in the air much the way a man could sense a well after spending much time in a desert. It had been a long time since he'd seen the ocean, and Clint was anxious to set his eyes upon all that sprawling blue with the spray upon his face.

The summer was wearing on, and Clint was getting used to the heat chewing at his skin. Spending so much time in the elements gave him a thicker hide than most, but that didn't make the blazing sun any easier to bear or the sweltering heat any cooler.

Clint leaned forward and patted his Darley Arabian stallion on the side of his neck. He'd gotten Eclipse a while ago from P. T. Barnum, during a stay in New York. Although he'd gotten close lately, Clint hadn't actually made his way back to that city. He was feeling a hankering for the ocean, but wasn't quite ready to dive into the teeming streets of a place so massive as New York City. After spending so long on the trail or in much smaller towns,

Clint got a bit overwhelmed at the thought of trading the clear, open skies for buildings on every side.

He wasn't exactly the skittish sort, so Clint figured that he would just put off his visit for a little while. That had been several miles and more than a few nights ago, however. In the time that had passed, Clint had been thinking about all that New York City had to offer. He'd even started to yearn for all the special comforts and excitement that only big-city life could offer.

At the moment, Clint was heading east through the state of New Hampshire. The land was green, and sprawled around him like a giant cloak of grass and trees. The air was alive with bits of pollen and the chirping of birds, as well as other things that weren't quite as easy to enjoy.

"What do you think, boy?" Clint asked the Darley Arabian. "You feel like paying a visit to your hometown?"

In response, Eclipse huffed and gave a loud snort. Clint didn't have to know what the horse was thinking to know what it meant. He was fairly certain that Eclipse wasn't even aware of the idle conversation coming from the man on his back. There were other things on the stallion's mind right then . . . several hundred of them, to be precise.

The gnats had been getting thicker along this particular stretch of road, and had become daring with their bigger numbers. Crawling over the stallion's hide like a living blanket, the bugs swirled around Eclipse's head and nibbled at his flesh.

Clint took his hat off and swiped at the bugs swarming around his face. "Anything would be a welcome change from dealing with these bugs, wouldn't it?"

Then again, having spent some time in the big city, Clint knew that New York was far from a pest-free environment. Scouting ahead with his eyes, Clint spotted a break in the trees that lined the trail on either side, and pressed his hat tightly against his head.

"All right," he said, taking firm hold of the reins. "Let's make a break for it."

Snapping the leather straps with a flick of his wrist, Clint lowered his head and got ready for the burst of speed that he knew would be coming. Eclipse didn't disappoint him, seeming all too eager to break out of his easy gait and into a full-out run.

The Darley Arabian thundered over the path and emerged from the trees like he'd been shot from a cannon. Leaves swirled in his path, and a cloud of dust was kicked up by Eclipse's pounding hooves as the horse charged into the more open country.

Once most of the trees were behind him, Clint pulled back on the reins. He did so mostly as a gentle warning to the animal rather than as an urgent command. Although he got the stallion to slow down a bit, Clint didn't insist on stopping until Eclipse had tired himself out a bit.

By the time the world had stopped speeding past him, Clint felt out of breath. "Damn, boy," he said, scratching Eclipse's ears. "And I wasn't even doing any of the running."

The stallion's sides were heaving and his breath came in healthy snorts. They'd left the swarm of gnats behind, which made everything else in the world a little easier to bear. Clint snapped the reins lightly against Eclipse's side, setting them off once again at a quick trot.

If he'd been a little closer to the city, Clint might have changed his mind right there and steered Eclipse toward New York. But he'd set his sights on a place a bit farther north, and was less than a day from that destination.

The place in Clint's sights was Coverdale, New Hampshire. In particular, there was a man by the name of Charlie Grayson who lived in Coverdale, and Clint figured he might as well look in on him as long as he was in this neck of the woods. Charlie was a good enough fellow, but Clint had other things in mind besides simply dropping in on an old friend.

The last time he'd seen him, Charlie ran a saloon in Coverdale called The Rusty Nail. Charlie had named the place because he always said a man never forgot stepping foot there. Clint had been to a lot of saloons in his day, but he couldn't disagree with Charlie's assessment of that one.

Not only was The Rusty Nail on the gamblers' circuit, but it also was one of the finest hotels in the state of New Hampshire. Several years ago, Clint had helped Charlie out of a very precarious position involving three women and a mad dog named Arlo McCree. Ever since then, Charlie said that Clint was always welcome in The Rusty Nail and wouldn't have to touch a bill.

Clint wasn't short on funds, especially after a recent healthy payday for a job in the Adirondacks, but he was curious as to how old Charlie was doing. That, combined with the fact that The Rusty Nail had built up some degree of fame in the area, made the prospect of taking a trip through Coverdale all the more appealing.

From there, Clint figured he might just keep riding east until he got a good look at the Atlantic. After that, New York City seemed to be the next reasonable destination.

At least . . . that was the plan. And if there was one thing in this world that Clint knew he could rely on, it was that plans had a nasty habit of getting changed.

Especially when those plans were made by The Gunsmith.

THREE

In Clint's experience, towns were a lot like trees. They either sprouted and grew or they withered away. In the case of Coverdale, New Hampshire, the former definitely seemed to be the case. The last time he'd been in the place, Coverdale was fairly good sized, with all the comforts of modern civilization. Now, Coverdale was a fully grown city. As for those comforts . . . Coverdale had at least four of each.

Riding past the city limits, Clint nodded in admiration at how things had changed since the last time he'd set foot on those streets. Some things looked vaguely familiar, but not many. There were a few business names that rang a bell in his mind, as well as a couple of street names, but only enough to let him know that he was in the right place.

The buildings and layout weren't the only things that had changed. There were also plenty more people and much more noise than what he remembered. Of course, it had been a long while since he'd been in those parts, and his memory was anything but perfect. Still, the place just felt different. It was too early to say if that was better or worse. It was just . . . different.

Clint swung his foot over Eclipse's back and dropped down from the saddle. Keeping hold of the reins, he led the Darley Arabian in the direction indicated by a sign that had the word "livery" painted in sloppy black letters. As soon as he turned a corner, Clint saw the wide-open doors of a stable set off the street on a small lot that was empty except for a pair of half-full troughs.

The moment Clint stepped through a gate that was tied open and entered the lot, a small, portly man waddled out of the stable, wiping his hands across the front of the battered apron he wore. Squinted eyes set into a chubby face sized Clint up in the time it took him to get to Eclipse, and a wide smile nearly broke his face in half.

"Hey, there," the liveryman said. "What can I do for you?"

Clint kept moving until he'd taken Eclipse in out of the blazing sun. "Got any empty stalls?"

Trailing behind Clint and Eclipse while swiping at the sweat on his brow, the liveryman moved so that he was once again in front of his newest customers. "For a fine animal like that one there, I'll make room."

"Glad to hear it."

"You wouldn't be willing to sell that there horse, would ya?"

The intense glare from Clint's sharp eyes was more than enough of an answer to put that particular question to rest.

"OK," the liveryman said while backpedaling a step or two. "You don't want to sell him. But I'll bet you want to make sure he gets the best care in town."

"You're right on that account."

"Then this is the place for you, mister. There ain't no one in Coverdale that knows horses like I do. They even run faster once they spend a night or two in my care."

Being a good judge of character was a skill that had

served Clint on more occasions than his ability with his modified Colt. Although he was fairly certain that the liveryman was familiar with how to stretch the truth a bit, he doubted he went any further than any other salesman. The squat man seemed to be into more than just feeding horses and cleaning stalls, but that wasn't necessarily a bad thing.

"All right," Clint said. "You sold me. How much?"

"A dollar a day."

Clint studied the man, giving him another taste of his intent stare.

"But for you . . . I'll make it half that. Providing you stay for at least four days, of course."

Clint acted like the price was more of an outrage than it was, and took out a silver dollar. "No guarantees on how long I'll be staying. But if the care's as good as you say, I'll make sure I don't take my business to one of the other places I passed on my way here."

"Fair enough."

After flipping the dollar into the liveryman's hand, Clint watched as Eclipse was led away and put into the closest stall. He had to admit that the place did seem pretty nice. It was clean and smelled of fresh hay, and the price was more than reasonable.

"What's your name, friend?" the liveryman asked.

"Clint Adams."

The man froze in place, his hand still resting on the door to Eclipse's stall. He cleared his throat and carried on as though he hadn't heard a thing. "I . . . may have heard of you. Is that Clint Adams . . . The Gunsmith?"

Rolling his eyes ever so slightly, Clint nodded. "Yeah. One and the same."

All pretense dropped away as the liveryman stumbled forward with his hand extended. "Abe Landon's my name. Great to meet you. I heard some stories from a man who came from Texas a couple months back that painted you in an impressive light. There's even a couple fellas in town that say they used to know you, but I never put much stock in what they said. Well . . . one of them's the sheriff, but you know how that goes. Anything to win an election, right?"

Abe jabbed his elbow into Clint's side as though they were sharing a joke over a mug of beer. Clint took it with a nod and stepped out of the other man's reach. "Yeah, right. So is The Rusty Nail still in business?"

"The Rusty Nail? Of course it is! As long as there's a Coverdale, there's going to be a Rusty Nail in it."

"Mind refreshing my memory on the quickest way to get there from here?"

Abe seemed to be lost in his own little world for the moment. He was looking straight at Clint, but not quite focusing on his face. "And here I thought all that was just talk."

"What's that?"

"When the sheriff said he knew you. I thought for sure that wasn't anything but loose talk."

"I don't know about the sheriff, but I can tell you that me and the owner of The Rusty Nail go a ways back."

Abe now stared at Clint as though he truly was looking at him. He blinked slowly, definite confusion written all over his face. "You . . . uhh . . . you're talking about the man that owns The Rusty Nail *saloon*, right?"

Clint looked back at him for a moment, not sure if Abe was going to bust out laughing or if he was just crazy after all. "Right. Charlie Grayson." Suddenly, Clint knew what was going on. In fact, he could see it written in Abe's features even better than the liveryman's confusion. "Or is that Sheriff Charlie Grayson?"

"That's what it would be, all right. You didn't know?"

"Believe me, if I would have known, I would have been

more than happy to avoid this whole conversation. How long has he been sheriff?"

"Going on a few months now." Abe scrunched his face up as though he'd suddenly aged a decade or so. "Or is that closer to a year? Whichever it is, he's been the law around here for a bit."

"And he still owns The Rusty Nail?"

"Couldn't live in that fancy house of his on just a lawman's salary," Abe replied with a sly wink. "And without all them free drinks to pass around, he wouldn't be half as popular."

"Speaking of free drinks, Sheriff Grayson owes me one or two. How about those directions?"

FOUR

"What the hell are you lookin' at?"

The man who'd been caught staring pulled his head back as though he'd been smacked on the nose. Reflexively, he shifted his eyes and took a few steps away. "Nothing. I wasn't looking at anything."

His upper lip curled in a snarl, Kevin Stohls kept his eyes trained on the other man until he could feel the tension crackling in the air. "Go on and spit it out, James. If I wanted to hear that kind of bootlicking, I'd ask any of the others what was on their shit-filled minds."

James was easily bigger than Stohls, standing no less than three or four inches over the other man. But despite the bulkier muscles and larger frame, James didn't have the imposing bearing that was as much a part of Stohls's nature as the black and gray-streaked hair on his head or the thick black beard covering his chin.

Physically, Stohls wasn't much to look at. He was average in many different ways, including his build and height. But there was something about him that was anything but average. It wasn't anything that could be readily seen or even touched, but it was something that could be sensed by anyone in his vicinity.

Kevin Stohls had a way about him that was imposing almost to the point of being intimidating, and he definitely could be intimidating when he chose. But that was reserved for those occasions when such a bearing was needed. Without having to try, Stohls was an imposing figure.

There was a darkness that surrounded him. It gave his eyes a sharp glint and made his whiskers seem like strands of ink. His features were just this side of pointed, making his face look like it had been cut from stone. He didn't look chiseled, however. In fact, he seemed to have been sculpted by a man in a rush, using a sledgehammer. When Stohls turned to look at someone, their first impulse was to look away. After all these years, Stohls was a master at using that effect of his appearance.

"You look anxious," Stohls said. "Go on and speak your mind."

"The rest of the gang ain't ready for this," James said. "Hell, we only just signed most of 'em on a few weeks ago."

"You don't think I know that? I was the one who found them."

"I've been with you on plenty of jobs, and you know that I'll cover your back if I'm able. And in all the years we've known each other, I can't remember saying this one time." James paused to swallow the knot that had been building in the back of his throat. He turned to look directly into Stohls's eyes, a feat that required a good amount of practice no matter how well he knew Kevin Stohls. "We're not ready to do this job. Trying now could be an awful big mistake."

Stohls was sitting on his horse with both hands resting on the saddle horn. Pulling in a breath until his lungs were full, he clenched his jaw shut and let out the air in a hiss. Turning so that he was no longer looking at the other man, he said, "We have known each other a long time, James. That's why I'll let you get away with saying what you just said to me."

"What I meant was—"

Stohls cut James off with a quickly raised hand. "I know what you meant. And no matter how long we've known each other, I'll tell you right now that I'll kill you quicker than you can blink if you tell another living soul what I'm about to say."

His eyes darting to and fro, glancing at the other men who were scattered in the distance, Stohls lowered his voice even though he would have had to scream to be heard by anyone else. "This job ain't supposed to work. Not as smoothly as they normally do, anyway."

"What?"

"You heard me. The law's been chewing on our heels for a while now. Any gambler worth his salt knows that a man can't buck the odds forever. We're set up for a fall. We got one coming, and there's no use in trying to dodge it any longer. We'd have to be fools to think we could keep raking in the money without having to pay our dues."

"But all we need to do is plan. Get some experience into these new men, and we'll be ready for bigger jobs again."

"Like that savings and loan in Albany? We were lucky to get out of there alive, and you know it. That bullet I took damn near crippled me."

"Yeah," James said. "*Almost.* We made it out of there with more cash than we could carry."

Stohls nodded slowly and pointed toward the group of men in the distance. There were seven of them scattered along the horizon, scouting ahead for campsites, their guns drawn and their nerves tighter than a bowstring. "Look at them, James. They're trying to find a place for us to sleep, but they might just as easily find a pack of deputies or bounty hunters who have been tracking us for God only knows how long."

"Occupational hazard. You told me that yourself."

"Right." Stohls laughed. "But the heat is getting too high. And when it burns for too long, sooner or later something starts to melt . . . or explode. Those men out there think we're like the Youngers or the Daltons. They think they're Billy the Kid, every last one of them. They're all actually just like them famous men. They're fools.

"Those others . . . just like those men right in front of us . . . thought they could beat the odds forever. Saloon owners get rich off that kind of thinking. But thieves and killers like us sure as hell don't. We only get our own selves killed."

"So what should we do?" James asked. "Ride out of here and head for Canada? We could probably make it."

"Then what? Retire? Hide for a while before skulking back into the States?"

"If you think we're headed for our graves, then I don't see how we have much choice."

"But there is a choice," Stohls whispered. "We can step up and take our fall like men. Get it out of the way and let the law think they've broken us for good. All we need to do is control the explosion. Then we can sit back and let all the heat burn itself away."

FIVE

The Rusty Nail was one of those places that was heard before it was seen. Following the instructions given to him by the liveryman, Clint crossed Driver's Avenue and was about to turn the corner onto Baltic when his ears picked out the sounds of voices and a piano blending together in a raucous mix.

He could only imagine how loud the place got once the sun went down, since the saloon he remembered had surely grown just like the town surrounding it. Before Clint got a chance to test that theory with his own eyes, however, he had to snap his mind back onto where he was going.

Coming around the corner, Clint came within less than an inch of plowing straight into a tall blonde woman who'd been striding with the same amount of purpose in her steps. They came face to face so quickly that each let out a surprised gasp and stared at the other with wide eyes.

Those wide, sky-blue eyes were all Clint could see for a moment. When he stepped back, he managed to get a look at the rest of the woman's face.

"Sorry about that," he said while reaching out to steady her by holding her arms. "I was in a bit of a hurry."

For a moment, the woman looked like she was mad enough to spit. After quickly looking Clint up and down, however, her expression lightened up and she even allowed herself to smile. "It's all right. I was in quite a rush myself."

"Are you all right?"

She nodded quickly. "Yeah. I'm fine."

Now that he'd had a chance to look at the rest of her, Clint could see that she was much more than fine. She was exquisite. Wearing a man's white cotton shirt wasn't nearly enough to conceal her large, rounded breasts. Her figure filled out the material as though the cotton fabric had been made to accentuate her curves. With the shirt tucked into her jeans, the line of her hips could be seen all the more clearly. She had the ripe, full-figured body of a woman blessed with natural beauty.

Her hair was a shadowy kind of blond that looked almost dark brown in certain places. It fell around her face in disorganized waves, giving her skin a coppery hue. Those blue eyes were set a little deeper into her face than most women's, giving her a darker quality that Clint couldn't help but find appealing. Before she spoke, her tongue slipped along full, rounded lips like a hint of things to come.

Taking in all of that with a glance, Clint found his eyes drawn to the gun at her side as another part of what attracted him. The pistol wasn't the dainty kind that most women carried if they decided to arm themselves. Instead, it was a .45 Smith & Wesson revolver that could very well blow a man's head off his shoulders.

The gun sat snugly in a holster that had been perfectly molded to her shapely figure after years of use. Every inch of leather was battered and worn, and every loop was filled with spare ammunition.

"Where were you headed in such a rush?" she asked.

"The Rusty Nail. I think it's just a little ways down Baltic, if I'm not mistaken."

"You're not mistaken. Just follow the sound of all those screamers and you won't miss it."

"Thanks." Clint stepped to one side and made a sweeping motion with his hand. "I won't keep you any longer than I have to, especially since I nearly knocked you off your feet."

She stood with one hand propped on her side and cocked her hips at an inviting angle. "Trying to get rid of me?"

"Nope. But if you don't move along quickly, I might not be able to let you go."

Smirking at the flirtation, she lowered her head for a moment. When she looked up again, she'd wiped the smile away and had put on a serious, no-nonsense expression. "And just how were you planning on keeping me from my business?"

When she asked that question, she made sure to let her hand slide over the edge of her pistol. Clint caught the motion instantly, not getting the least bit of threat from it. "By buying you a drink. Something tells me that you wouldn't turn your nose up at an offer like that."

"Do I look like a drunk?"

"No. You look like you wouldn't mind spending a little more time with me."

She tried to keep her expression stern and her eyes hard. No matter how much effort she put into it, however, she couldn't manage to keep up the facade for more than a couple of seconds. Finally, her lips curved into a warm smile and she let out the laugh she'd been holding back.

"Should I take that to mean that I'm right?" Clint asked, even though he already knew the answer.

The woman took her hand off her gun and held it out to Clint. "You certainly can. My name's Willa Singer."

"That's an unusual name, Willa."

"It's short for Wilhelmina, but if I catch you calling me that, I'll be forced to shoot you after all."

Clint shook her hand, admiring the strength in her grip. "I wouldn't dare take you up on that offer," he said without a hint of sarcasm. "I'm Clint. And that would be short for Clint Adams."

"Will you be at The Rusty Nail for long, Clint Adams?"

"Possibly."

"Then I'll meet you there in a bit. I've still got some errands to run, but I'll be sure to head back this way once they're done. If I don't see you again, it's sure been nice running into you."

Clint tipped his hat and said, "Same here."

Willa turned and started in the same direction she'd been going. She quickly gathered all the steam that had carried her around the corner when Clint first laid eyes on her, only this time he was in a position to enjoy it a whole lot more. Each of her steps caused her hips to move back and forth, drawing Clint's attention to her plump, muscular buttocks.

"The pleasure was all mine," he said to himself before continuing toward the saloon.

SIX

James looked at the other men the way that Stohls was doing. They all seemed to be doing their jobs well enough, and had already proven themselves worthy to join the gang. But Stohls had never really treated them like his equals. James saw that especially clearly with Stohls's recent words still fresh in his mind.

"They're cattle," Stohls said simply. "They're lambs who fancy themselves as wolves. And the best thing to do to lambs is lead them to the slaughter."

James felt his stomach tighten, and a wave of damp cold swept over him. "So what do you propose? Turn them in? Cut them loose from the gang and let the law have them?"

"Better than that. I propose we give the law exactly what they want. And at the same time, we take the heat off and pull some of those odds back into our favor." The smile on Stohls's face was barely more than a shift of his lips, but it was one of the biggest grins he'd ever worn in his life. "We go through with this job and lead our lambs to their slaughter."

"You mean kill those men?"

"Think of it as shaving the fat from our group. If the law gets some kills under their belts, they'll be happy for a while. And if they're happy for a while, we can slip away with the money we get from this job."

"So you still want to go through with this job?"

"Of course. And since we won't mind losing most of our little sheep in the process, we shouldn't have any trouble at all getting our hands on that money. You know just as well as I do that the hardest part of any robbery is getting out with your skin intact. Stop worrying about that and the rest is a cakewalk."

James shook his head. "I don't like it. This all sounds crazy to me."

"Crazy?" Stohls's tone was cold as the grave. "How much longer do you think we can do this, James? How much longer until we catch a bullet from some punk deputy who gets lucky? Or some bounty hunter who spots us crossing a street somewhere?"

"That can happen just as easily after we give the law this fall of yours. You've got to know that."

"Sure. But the odds won't be so stacked against us. Especially when they think we're dead."

Now James had the feeling that he'd hit the true meaning of this conversation. "Say that again."

Stohls was staring straight into the other man's face. His eyes were narrow and glimmering with a familiar internal light. "The last notice we saw . . . back in Charleston, I think it was . . . how much was the reward for our heads?"

"Upward of fifteen thousand for us two. Maybe more."

"And how big was our gang back then?"

"There were seven of us. We joked that we were each worth only a little more than two thousand a piece."

Stohls grinned again, taking on the appearance of a fox that had just stuck his nose into a henhouse. "And so far, there's no way for anyone to know about these new men we took on after parting company with Deke and the rest. That means the law still thinks there's seven of us total. So all we have to do is make this fall look good enough and make sure it hits hard enough. Because if we do that part right, we'll be able to ride away from this next job without a care in the world. After all . . . the law don't waste its time tracking down dead men."

When he looked at the rest of the gang, James felt as though a veil had been lifted from his eyes. Now, rather than just the seven other men who were riding with him and Stohls, James saw another vision. He saw the *entire* gang. "So as far as the law is concerned, they won't have killed just some of us. Or even just most of us."

"All of us," Stohls finished. "They'll think they got all of us. I'm thinking a fire would be good enough to pull off that job. I could set it, and once they pull enough bodies out of the flames, they'll think they rid the world of another evil and go about their stupid lives."

"You really think it'll work?" James asked, looking away from the seven others. "You really think they'll believe we're dead? Or what about those men out there? You think they'll go along with this?"

"Those men'll do what they're told . . . just like the perfect little sheep they are. And the law aren't anything but regular folks with a star pinned to their chests. They're stupid and lazy. All they want is to get their jobs done and go home to stuff some dinner in their faces and stick their dicks into a woman. Not only will they believe this, but they'll try to look like heroes in the process of selling it to everyone else.

"All we'll have to do is slip away in the confusion while the law goes around taking down all of those posters with our names on them. We can split the money two ways instead of nine. What do you say?"

James mulled the proposition, turning it over and over inside his head like a man admiring a piece of gold he'd just pulled from a muddy riverbank. At first, it had seemed like nothing more than a sloppy mess. But now that he'd wiped away some of the grime, he could actually see the glittering treasure underneath.

After working with more than his fair share of wanted men, James knew that they were always looking for a way to line their pockets. Even after the biggest imaginable scores, thieves were always trying to get richer and killers were always trying to get more blood on their hands. Because of that, the minds of such men were always working in an attempt to improve their position.

If the plan had come from anyone else, James wouldn't have thought it had a chance of working. Not a chance in hell. In fact, James might have considered doing away with the man who'd thought of such a thing out of sheer principle.

But Kevin Stohls didn't think like other men. James knew that for a fact. Stohls had a knack for pulling off things that had no business working. He found ways around dead ends, and he could wring hope from dirty burlap. If anyone could pull off a switch on this scale, it would be Kevin Stohls. James was certain of that.

He was also certain of something else. Too much time had gone by without any words to fill the empty air.

Sure enough, when James glanced over to Stohls's hand, he found it drifting toward one of the twin .44s holstered at Stohls's hip. It wasn't much more than a subtle movement of less than a quarter of an inch . . . not enough to cause anyone else to suspect a thing. And that, James knew, was exactly what Stohls counted on.

"What do you think?" Stohls asked. "You want to give this a go?"

The wrong words at this moment, even a wayward

twitch, and James was certain he'd be dead. Death might have come right then or a little later, when he let his guard down, but it would come. There was no mistaking it. But it would come only if James said the wrong thing or made the wrong move.

He didn't have to worry about either of those things.

Shaking his head, James felt a grin swelling up inside of him, and let it spread out across his face. "Let's do it."

"Now that's what I wanted to hear," Stohls said without taking his hand away from his gun. "I wasn't sure which way you were going to jump."

"Neither was I, to be honest. I think you missed your calling, old friend. You should've been a salesman."

"Nah. Salesmen don't get to have half the fun we do."

SEVEN

The last time Clint had walked through the door of The Rusty Nail, the knob had fallen off in his hand. The saloon had never been a total dive, but its owner was more concerned with what went on inside than the condition of its outside. People had always been in the place, but it had been rough and chaotic at best.

Now, Clint had to look twice before believing that he had indeed found the right place. Not only was The Rusty Nail sporting clean walls and a monstrously huge new front window, but the entrance had been widened to twice its original size and the plain door was now a set of bat wings. The most striking thing, however, was the fact that The Rusty Nail had grown upward rather than out, sporting a brand-new second floor.

"Jesus, Joseph, and Mary," Clint said after a low whistle.

He was impressed with what he saw, but a little overwhelmed as well. If the outside was so drastically different, he could hardly imagine what the place looked like beyond those bat-wing doors. His curiosity was great enough to overcome anything else he might have been feeling. And it was that, combined with a suddenly growing thirst, that drove Clint through those doors almost as fast as he'd been going when he'd run into Willa Singer.

The doors swung open soundlessly on well-oiled hinges. They slapped together much like their namesake after Clint walked through, only to swing open again as someone else walked in a moment later. Clint looked around at all the polished wood and spit-shined chrome. The place looked so clean that it might have been built a week ago. It seemed like a shame to walk across such a perfectly maintained floor.

But Clint wasn't the type to stand by when there was a perfectly good saloon right in front of him. Especially when that saloon was as perfectly good as The Rusty Nail. Returning the nods and greetings from some of the other drinkers leaning against the bar, Clint made his way to the closest tender and set one foot upon the shining rail.

"What'll it be, mister?" the man behind the bar asked. He was balding and looked to be in his late fifties. Sweat glistened on the bare spots of his scalp and stained the pits of his shirt. Compared with everything else in the place, the men working at the bar seemed to be the least cared for.

"I'll have a beer," Clint said. "As well as a talk with the man who owns this place."

Already holding an empty mug beneath one of many taps, the bartender snapped his chin up and looked at Clint with a surprised expression. "There a problem?"

"Not yet."

"Something I can help ya with? Maybe one of our girls can put you in a better mood."

"I don't want to complain. I just want to talk to Charlie. Is he around?"

Now the barkeep's expression drifted more toward suspicious. His eyes narrowed slightly, and he turned as though trying to look at another part of the room without letting Clint out of his sight. "Sheriff Grayson, you mean? He's around here somewhere."

"Then point me in the right direction. I'm an old friend of his. The name's Clint Adams."

For a second, the barkeep looked like he was about to break out in laughter. Then, once he got a closer look at Clint's face and could tell that he was dead serious, he jumped back almost hard enough to spill the beer he'd just poured. "Clint Adams! I'll be damned. That really *is* you, isn't it?"

"Last time I checked."

"Shit, if I'd known it was you, I never would've given you such a hard time. Lots of folks come stumbling in here asking to see Sheriff Grayson, but they're not the type to be trusted." Suddenly, the barkeep snapped his mouth shut. "That's not to say you're not to be trusted. Or that you were stumbling in here. Or even that—"

"It's all right. Just tell me where Charlie's at, and you can take a breath."

That seemed to put the barkeep at ease just enough for him to lower his shoulders from up around his ears. Letting out a relieved breath, he pointed toward the back of the room. "Over there. He's playing cards with some of his investors."

Clint glanced in that direction. There were too many card tables for him to pick out the correct one right away, but there weren't so many as to make the search impossible. Taking his drink and flipping a coin onto the bar, Clint turned and headed toward the gambling area.

"Mister Adams," the barkeep shouted.

Without stopping, Clint looked over his shoulder.

The barkeep held up the coin and flipped it through the air. "If Sheriff Grayson heard that I took your money, I'd be out on my ear."

Seeing that the coin was headed straight for his mug, Clint twisted at the waist and managed to catch the coin with his other hand half a second before the money landed in his beer. He returned the bartender's enthusiastic wave and continued toward the back of the room.

By the time he could overhear some of the conversations going on in the various card games, Clint noticed a change in the entire atmosphere. While the rest of the saloon was brimming with chatter and noise, the section designated for gambling was more subdued, if not quiet. The players spoke only loud enough to be heard, and the drunks were ushered away from the games before they could make a nuisance of themselves. Even the servers and entertaining girls made their rounds a little more carefully. Apparently gambling was a serious business at The Rusty Nail.

Clint was glad to see that some things never changed.

Of course, when he finally spotted Charlie Grayson sitting with his back against the farthest wall, Clint realized that other things not only had changed . . . they had been re-created from the bottom up.

EIGHT

"What the . . . ?" Charlie Grayson's head snapped back, and he nearly dropped the cards he was holding. "Is that you, Clint?"

"It sure is. How the hell have you been?"

Charlie slapped his cards facedown on the table and pushed his chair back so he could get up. The instant he was on his feet, he rushed around the table with his arms open. "It's been a hell of a long time, Adams!" Charlie embraced Clint in a brotherly hug, slapping him on the back with both hands before stepping back again.

Clint didn't remember Charlie as a terribly big man, but he seemed to have grown since the last time. He certainly didn't recall being so close to him, and barely knew how to react when Grayson nearly bear-hugged the stuffing out of him.

"You sure have changed," Clint said, expressing the one thought that pulsed through his brain.

"The years have been kind, that's for sure. Can I get you a drink?"

Holding up his mug, Clint saw that it was now half-empty. Besides that, his sleeve and shirt were wet. "I had a drink, Charlie. Or at least I did before you mauled me."

Charlie glanced down and laughed. "Sorry 'bout that. Let me top that off for ya."

Following Grayson back toward the bar, Clint noticed that he had gone through a near-total metamorphosis. The man had once been a soft-spoken saloon owner who knew how to talk to just about anyone over a drink. Now Charlie walked like he was king of the mountain, strutting through The Rusty Nail as if he owned not only it, but the rest of the town besides. Everyone they passed seemed to be under that impression as well, stepping aside and greeting him with a quick, respectful word as Grayson moved on.

Once they were at the bar, Charlie guided Clint to the farthest end, where there was hardly anyone standing. "Give the man another drink," Grayson said to the barkeep. "And a towel."

"Yes, sir, Sheriff," the bartender said, then scuttled off to fill Grayson's requests.

"So what brings you back to Coverdale?"

"I was passing by," Clint said. "After spending some time in the mountains, I decided to swing through here and check up on an old friend. Tell you the truth, I'm surprised I even recognized you."

The barkeep set a fresh beer in front of Clint, dropping a folded gray rag down next to it. He was gone the next instant, quickly finding something else to do well out of earshot.

Charlie puffed out his chest and lifted his chin a little. Dressed in a pressed white shirt beneath a black waistcoat, he looked more like a gambler than a lawman. Of course, the badge pinned to his lapel was pretty hard to miss. Clint spotted a gun belt around his waist, but couldn't see what kind of iron Grayson was packing. The holster looked hardly creased, however, which told Clint quite a bit.

"Last time you saw me, I was just a saloon keeper, wasn't I?"

Clint nodded. "This place was still one of the best around."

"Yeah, but now it's better. And because of that, I was able to hear a nice little bit of information that landed me my very first arrest."

After one sip, Clint realized that the beer wasn't good. It was damn near perfect. He couldn't help but glance down at the mug in admiration before turning his attention back to Grayson. "Your first arrest?"

"Yep. Even before I got elected sheriff. They call that a citizen's arrest." Charlie said that last part like a proud child showing off what he'd learned at school earlier in the day. "It was connected to a robbery at a store here in town. Someone drinking here knew who it was, so I got him drunk and he spilled the whole story. I arrested him later that day."

Clint froze with his mug halfway to his mouth. His eyes locked onto Charlie's and narrowed slightly. When he cocked his head just enough, he could see uncertainty appearing on Charlie's face like cracks in a dam.

"All right," Charlie said. "Me and some of the fellas I employ went to make the arrest. They work security at my place."

Clint kept his eyes right where they were. He knew Charlie had changed, but didn't figure that anyone could change *that* much. Either that, or Clint's ability to size up other people was seriously slipping.

"All right, *all right,*" Charlie moaned. "Me, some of my security workers, and a deputy or two. But I got all the credit and it was me that got the information."

Smirking, Clint took a drink from his mug and turned the intensity in his eyes down a notch. "That's more like the Charlie I knew."

"And what's that supposed to mean?"

"It means that the Charlie I knew was so busy trying to get on the good sides of three women at one time that he damn near let Arlo McCree walk right in and have a drink fresh from robbing the bank in a town less than five miles away."

"I can't recognize every criminal type that walks in here."

"He was sitting next to his own wanted poster."

"People come in all the time and tack those things to the wall. . . ."

"You had put it up just ten minutes before McCree walked in."

"How do you know so damn much?"

"Because I helped you do it," Clint answered. "And if you'd have been paying attention to a little detail like a killer and thief walking into your place, you might not have gotten yourself in that jam I had to get you out of."

Charlie's first reaction was to jump to his own defense. He opened his mouth and started to make a noise that sounded like the beginning of a boisterous response to what Clint had said. But before he could get out much more than a squeak, he deflated like a bellows that had all the air sucked out of it.

"Dammit, Clint. Keep your voice down, will ya?"

"*There's* the Charlie Grayson I remember. How've you been?"

NINE

Seven men rode into Coverdale as the sun was being absorbed by the western sky. The light of day was quickly becoming a memory as the last rays of light shot out like a dying wail. It was the time of day when everything was hard to see if you were looking anywhere but away from the sunset. The light seemed to stab into every eye it could, washing out all but basic shapes in a brilliant glare.

It was instinct for folks to turn their heads down and keep their eyes shielded during those last few minutes of the day. Those who didn't, kept their eyes squinted so tightly that they were forced to look at the world through slits. Even the men who were used to the light in their eyes found themselves blinded every once in a while.

That was just the way it was at that time of day.

And that was why Stohls had chosen that particular time to make his entrance into town.

The guy riding at the head of the pack kept his shoulders hunched just as he'd been instructed. As much as he wanted to straighten up and show his pride at being chosen by the leader of the gang himself, he kept his posture stooped and his hat pulled low over his face.

That man rode ahead of the rest of the first group, leading the newest members of the gang into Coverdale while Stohls and James came in a little way behind. It was an honor to ride in at the fore. At least, that's what James had told him. That way, all the new members could prove themselves at once.

Stohls wouldn't be there to call the shots. And if everything went well enough, the new members would get a bigger share of the profits as well as the respect of the two founding fathers. Stohls didn't give his respect easily, which was why obtaining that prize was first in the minds of all seven of that first group.

After that job, they knew they would be genuine bad men.

They would be on their way to money and infamy.

With all of this firmly in mind, the seven men rode down Coverdale's main street, heading straight for the savings and loan that was to be their target. None of the riders got more than a sideways glance from any of the locals. In fact, some of them got a friendly wave or two. The riders smiled at that, laughing among themselves at just how easy this was all going to be.

The man at the head of the group straightened up a little in his saddle. He couldn't help it. Everything was getting so close. Before he knew it, he would be riding out with everything he'd been wanting. All seven of them would, for that matter.

Money and infamy.

All ripe for the picking.

Looking through a dented telescope, James shook his head and made a low grumbling sound in the back of his throat.

"What's the matter?" Stohls asked as he splashed water on his face. "You having second thoughts?"

"No."

"Then why are you making noises over there like a mother hen?"

James lowered the spyglass, but kept his eyes trained in the same direction he'd been looking. The two men were sitting on their horses near a lot on the outskirts of town. There was the skeletal beginning of a building there, but the workers had gone home for the day.

"I just can't believe that this is going so easily," James said. "I mean, we change our routine, give them the story about proving themselves, make them ride in alone on such a big job, and they didn't even suspect a thing? I'm not sure. . . ."

Leaning over to snatch the telescope from James's hand, Stohls said, "There's no reason for them not to believe us. Besides . . . as long as they do what they're told for the next couple of minutes, it won't matter what the hell they believe."

After watching through the glass for a few seconds, Stohls snapped it shut and handed it back to James. "They're in," he said.

James nodded appreciatively. "Then it looks like they're going for it after all. Are we just going to leave them to it?"

"You know better than that," Stohls said with a sideways glance. "That would only be leaving an opening for something to go wrong. Most folks are too stupid to do anything the right way without someone there to hold their hand. If we leave them to it, all that'll happen is they'll get their heads blown off before everything falls into place.

"We'll be heading in, all right. In fact . . . it's about time for us to do that right now."

Stohls jabbed his spurs into his horse's sides, sending the beast jolting off at a quick pace. James snapped the reins and fell in next to his partner as they bolted down the street and into the more crowded section of Coverdale. They rode with speed and purpose, sending locals scattering for cover as they thundered by without a care for anything or anyone around them.

The group of riders was still a ways ahead of them, approaching the savings and loan at the other end of town. As they reached the corner of Third and Baltic, James and Stohls parted ways. James veered off to the left while Stohls continued straight on.

Both men were experts at the craft of deception, and knew exactly when to slow their horses rather than draw unwanted attention to themselves. As the number of milling locals and the horse traffic increased, the outlaws all but disappeared into the crowd, allowing themselves to be swallowed whole.

Stohls would have grinned if any of this would have come as a surprise. But he'd seen all of this as though it had already happened. Those seven men, like the rest of the population, were stupid and easy to read. Any man who knew that could manipulate those people using the same bait and tactics that would work with any other dumb animal.

Bait and switch.

It was so easy that Stohls nearly considered that to be more of a crime than killing or stealing. Then again . . . the way he thought of it . . . him being above the rest of the herd gave him certain privileges. Slaughtering and shearing the sheep. That's all it was. And that had never been a crime.

TEN

Once he'd broken through the sheriff's defenses and gotten him away from what seemed to be an adoring public, Clint didn't have much trouble getting down to the real Charlie Grayson. It wasn't too long before Charlie was laughing and joking just like old times. They swapped stories and caught up on each other's news. Clint had a sneaking suspicion that most of Charlie's stories were a little more fiction than he was letting on.

Even so, Clint enjoyed the tales. Exaggerations or not, Charlie's stories were amusing. Before Clint knew it, the light streaming in through the front window was turning bright orange and then dark red.

Charlie winced and shaded his eyes with his hand. "Looks like it's getting dark."

"I was just noticing that," Clint said. "What time is it?"

"It's about time for you to make good on that drink you owe me."

Clint and Charlie turned to get a look at who had just spoken. Although the light was making it somewhat difficult to see details, there was no mistaking the cascading blonde hair or the curvaceous figure.

Clint stepped forward as Willa Singer came to stand between him and Charlie. She was still dressed in her jeans and man's shirt, but she looked better than some of the saloon girls who were wearing their finest to attract potential customers.

"I was wondering if you were going to show," Clint said. The smell from Willa's hair was a mixture of summer air and her own natural scent. She returned his smile and settled close enough for her hand to brush against the top of his thigh.

"I wasn't about to go off without paying you a visit," she said. "Besides . . . I never turn down a free drink."

Charlie grinned and nodded. "Spoken just like a lady."

Willa faced Grayson with a quick turn of her head. "I'd be offended by that remark if it wasn't true. But, then again, you'd know all about having to bribe women with drinks to earn their favor."

Clint chuckled to himself and held his hands up when Charlie looked to him for support.

"You got me there, ma'am," Grayson said. "I hope I won't have to resort to such measures to keep your pretty little self around here for a bit."

"Well," she said, tilting her head in a way she knew to be damn near irresistible to men. "You could always arrest me."

Charlie was unable to find the right words for a moment. Apparently he couldn't decide whether or not she was being serious. Either that, or he just found himself flustered when he got too good a look at Willa Singer.

Savoring the moment for a bit while Clint looked on, Willa smiled before letting Charlie off the hook. "Before you get your tongue too tied, there's something else you should tend to, Sheriff."

"Oh. Uh . . . what's that?"

"Someone wants to see you," she said. "He was asking

for you at the front of the bar when I walked in." Turning so that her proud breasts were displayed perfectly, she pointed toward the other end of the room. "That's him. The one who looks like he's about to bust."

Pulling himself together, Charlie straightened his coat and cleared his throat. "He does look riled up about something. I'll see to it. Don't go anywhere, ma'am. I'll be right back."

Willa didn't even try to look impressed as Grayson tipped his hat and shoved his way through the crowd. "He doesn't seem like the law dog type."

"You got that right," Clint said.

"And neither do you. I had you figured for more of the solitary kind. You know . . . sitting by yourself . . . maybe playing some cards."

"You've got me all figured, huh?"

"I thought so. Then I come and find you rubbing shoulders with the sheriff. Imagine my surprise."

"Disappointed?"

"No. But I will be if you don't come a little closer."

Clint stepped up to her until there was only an inch separating them. Her smell was enveloping him now, digging into the center of his body and stirring up all kinds of desires. When he looked into her eyes, he could see that same kind of intensity swirling inside of Willa. She looked excited and anxious, nibbling on her full bottom lip while pulling in a quick breath.

"I'm here," Clint said. "Now what?"

"Now how about that drink?"

"I don't think so."

She raised her eyebrow and cocked her head slightly. The movement brought her mouth just a little bit closer to his. "I also had you figured for a man who follows through on what he starts."

"I follow through. But I think I'd like to start something else."

Before she could get another word out, Willa felt Clint's mouth on her lips. She pressed her body against him, running her hands along the outsides of his legs before reaching around to grab hold and pull him even closer.

Although Clint had Willa figured for an aggressive woman, he didn't know just how aggressive she was until he felt her groping him right there at the bar. Her hands were warm and strong, and they were rubbing him in all the right places, so he wasn't about to pull them away. Instead, he let his hands do some wandering of their own.

He could feel the taut muscles of her stomach through her shirt. From there, it was a short trip up to run his fingers along the sides of her breasts.

"I want you," she whispered into Clint's ear. "I want you right here. Right now."

ELEVEN

Her fingers were already working at unfastening his pants. Clint could feel her hand touching the skin beneath his belt, slipping under the layers of clothing and working toward the bulge at his crotch.

It took every ounce of his strength to keep himself from picking Willa up, setting her on the bar, and ripping every stitch of clothing from her body. At that moment, everyone else inside the crowded saloon no longer seemed to matter. Clint couldn't even hear their voices over the rush of blood thrumming in his veins. He did, however, back Willa up so that they were in a darker corner, where the bar met the wall, instead of out in plain sight. This was unlike anything he'd ever done with a woman before . . . which, of course, made it all the more exciting.

Once she had his jeans undone, Willa backed up so that she was leaning against the bar. Clint kept himself close to her and stood with his back to the rest of the room and one foot propped up on the brass rail near the floor.

Neither of them spoke. They simply let their eyes wander up and down one another's body, their breath rushing in and out in shallow bursts. Willa's hands were still busy, this time loosening her own clothes. With a few twists of her wrists, the front of her jeans was open and she was pulling them down just far enough for Clint to see the upper edge of the dark thatch of hair between her legs.

As much as he hated to admit it, Clint was suddenly very much aware of where they were and what they were doing. "I need to get you to a room," he said.

"What's the matter?" Willa's voice was tense and teasing at the same time. "You scared of what people might think? You nervous about attracting the attention of a bunch of drunks and gamblers?"

Her body felt soft and strong beneath his hands. Every once in a while, Clint got a sample of her smooth skin as his fingers brushed along a part of her that was exposed. Those were only brief tastes, however, since her bare skin was peeking out in slivers between pushed-aside articles of clothing.

Pushing his hips against Willa, Clint made sure his erection was rubbing directly between her legs. Even through the layers of clothing, the sensation was exhilarating enough to cause their breaths to catch in their throats.

"The only thing I'm nervous about right now," he said, "is getting arrested for fucking you right in front of all these drunks and gamblers. But give me another couple of seconds, and I'll get over that."

Willa reacted to Clint's rough words as though he'd managed to slip inside of her. She smiled, baring her teeth at the same time, locking her eyes onto Clint with such power that he couldn't move away from her even if he'd wanted to.

"You won't get arrested," Willa said. "The sheriff looks like he'll be busy for a while yet."

Dragging his eyes away from her for the briefest of seconds, Clint glanced toward the front of the bar where

Charlie had gone. Grayson was involved in a heated conversation and seemed to be about to walk through the front door. Suddenly, Charlie looked straight back at Clint and lifted a hand in a quick wave.

Clint would have returned the gesture, but one of his hands was on Willa's smooth backside while the other was in the hot patch between her legs. So he simply nodded, and that seemed to satisfy Charlie. The sheriff pointed toward the door and then headed through it.

There were plenty of people still milling around the saloon. While most of them seemed accustomed to giving the back of the bar a wide berth, that didn't mean they pretended it didn't exist.

"Looks like it's just you and me now," she said.

Catching more than one local glancing toward him before looking quickly away, Clint answered, "Not hardly."

"Then I guess I'll just stop this." Keeping her eyes focused on Clint's, Willa slid her hand further between his legs, massaging the bulge of his cock through his pants. Her smile grew when she felt him get harder. "Somehow I get the impression that you don't want me to stop."

Although Clint had been thinking about renting one of the rooms upstairs, he was having a difficult time getting himself to suggest moving away from the spot where they were standing. Willa's hands worked him so well that he didn't even want to shift on his feet. She seemed to feel the same way as he slid his fingers a little farther down the front of her pants until he found the hard little nub of her clitoris.

He kept his finger pressed on her sensitive little button and made little circles, smiling as he saw that he was inflicting just as much pleasure on her as she was on him.

TWELVE

"What the hell is going on here?" Sheriff Grayson blustered.

The man he was speaking to winced slightly, but it was more of a reaction to the loudness of the lawman's voice rather than any intimidation that Charlie was trying to put into it. "I got a tip from someone that I thought you might want to hear," he said. "So I came to get you. Were you doing anything important?" The tone in the man's voice betrayed the fact that he already knew the answer to that question.

Charlie took a breath and patted the other man on the shoulder. "No. Just catching up with an old friend. Sorry about being cross with you, Mark."

"That's all right," Mark answered dryly. "Do you want to talk to this fella or not?"

"Which fella?"

"The one with the tip. He said he saw something suspicious."

"Oh, yeah. Sure. Where is he?"

Mark rolled his eyes the moment his back was turned to the sheriff. If it wasn't for the deputy badge pinned to his own chest, he might have told Grayson what he thought of him some time ago. "Right over here." He led Grayson across the street to an anxious-looking older man dressed in simple, dark clothes.

The man looked as though he could hardly stay in one spot, and the moment he spotted the badges headed in his direction, he all but jumped out of his skin. His hair was partly gray, and his skin looked like leather that had seen better days. His face was sunken, grizzled, and marked by little cuts that ran down his neck. "I saw 'em, Sheriff. I saw all of 'em riding into town. There was at least seven of 'em. Maybe more."

Grayson put on his most official-looking expression and propped both hands upon his hips. "Now just calm down, sir. Take a breath and tell me exactly what you saw." His voice was calm and level.

The man's eyes darted back and forth, and he pointed down the street with a trembling finger. "They came in from the west. They all rode in a group and headed straight through town."

"And what makes you think that they're not here for a drink or a place to stay?"

For a moment, the older man kept quiet. His mouth moved, but nothing came out as he looked away from Grayson and toward the man standing beside him. Mark stood there with his arms crossed until he saw that he was being sought out.

"Just tell Sheriff Grayson what you told me," Mark said. "It's all right."

"It's not all right," the other man said. "I can sure as hell tell you that much."

Grayson leaned closer and sniffed the air in front of the nervous man's face. "Have you been drinking?"

"No, goddammit! I wasn't drinking nothing. I was just coming out of the barbershop down on Third when I saw 'em all riding in just as proud as you please." Once the man got going, words flew out of his mouth in a frenzied rush. "The minute I saw these men, I could tell they were up to no good. They had that look about them, you know?"

Rubbing his chin, Grayson asked, "Were they armed?"

"To the teeth. I could see pistols on their hips, but more than that, they had shotguns chucked over their shoulders. They looked like the type that would use 'em, too! I've done some bounty hunting in my day, and I know how to tell men who carry guns from men who use them. These were users if I ever saw one."

"Where were they headed?"

"Toward the savings and loan. Soon as I saw that, I headed straight down here to let you know."

Clenching his jaw, Grayson took on the look of someone who felt guilty for something he was about to do. He took a deep breath and hooked his thumbs through his gun belt. "Maybe it's nothing."

"Or maybe it's a gang of robbers," Mark cut in.

Grayson pulled Mark aside and lowered his voice so the older man couldn't hear. "Do you know this man?"

Mark shrugged. "I might've seen him around once or twice, but I couldn't say for sure."

"Should we listen to what he's saying?"

"It's worth a look. Of course, if we put it off much longer, we might as well not even bother."

Grayson nodded, and let out the breath he'd been holding. "All right," he said sternly. "I'll go check it out. Mark, gather some of the other boys and meet me down at the savings and loan."

"I want to go, too."

The two lawmen couldn't believe their ears.

"I told you I did some bounty hunting," the older man

said defensively. "Even know my way around my own gun."

Mark studied him with narrowed eyes. "Do you really think you could be a help?"

"Hell, yes. But more'n that . . . if these men are robbers and they get caught here today off'a something I reported . . . I want to be in on it. And I want to get a piece of any reward that's coming."

"What do you think, Sheriff?"

"Whatever," Grayson said, waving his hand dismissively. "I've got bigger problems right now. Just make sure he doesn't get in the way. And hurry up with the rest of those deputies. I don't want to be there too long all by mys—" He stopped himself right there and cleared his throat. "That is . . . if there's seven of them, I want to meet them with men to back me up. That's just the smart way to go about this."

"Yeah, Sheriff. It sure is."

His point made, Grayson slapped the gun at his hip as if to make sure the weapon was still there, then started down the street. Mark watched him go and rolled his eyes the way he always did whenever he saw the town's newest sheriff trying to act official.

"What did you say your name was?" Mark asked the other man.

"Eldon. Eldon Masters."

"If you really know how to use that gun of yours, you might as well come with me, Eldon. I have a feeling we're going to need all the help we can get."

THIRTEEN

"Maybe we should go somewhere we can be alone," Clint said.

Willa's eyes rolled up into her head and she drew in a deep breath. Letting it out with a strained sigh, she said, "I told you . . . I want you . . . right here and . . . right now."

Clint felt a few gentle tugs, and before he knew what was going on, Willa's hand was closing around his bare penis. Moving in a little closer to keep the sight from prying eyes, Clint untucked his shirt and let the front tails hang down like a makeshift screen.

The moment he'd somewhat shielded their lower bodies from view, Clint felt the tip of his cock brush up against hot, moist skin. His eyes grew a little wider, and when he looked at Willa, she was staring straight at him with a challenging smirk.

"You weren't kidding, were you?" Clint said.

"Nope. When I want something . . . I grab it." She punctuated those last three words by clasping her hand around Clint's penis and moving it along the slit between her legs. She didn't put him inside of her, but instead rubbed the head of his cock up and down over the lips of her pussy.

No matter how many people were looking, Clint wanted to plunge himself deeply into her. In fact, the notion that so many people could be watching was so outlandish that it heightened all the sensations that were coursing through his body.

"I see a room back there," she said, nodding toward an unmarked door no more than twenty feet away along the back wall. "I say we—"

"Oh, no, you don't," Clint snapped. "Right here. Right now. *That's* what you said."

She was still holding him between her legs, and all it took was a quick thrust of his hips for Clint to push inside of her. Willa responded with a look of shock that quickly turned into something even more than the start of an orgasm. Her eyes were wide, and her mouth fell open as she let out a loud moan that she quickly pushed back down inside of her.

Clint was in her for only a moment before he pulled out again, his cock still moving between her fingers.

With one hand, Clint took hold of one of Willa's legs, lifted it and moved it to one side. He set it down so that her foot was on the rail and he could step even closer.

She let out a low purring sound that only Clint could hear. While she did that, Willa lowered her head so that she could nibble on Clint's neck as she shifted so that his penis fit inside of her. When Clint didn't push all the way in, she moved her hips forward until her lips were wrapped around him.

Clint glanced around, trying to keep a casual look upon his face. Most of the people weren't paying them any mind. The bartender caught Clint's eye and gave him a questioning look. When Clint shook his head that he didn't want another drink, the barkeep turned his attention back to other customers.

Looking down, Clint saw that they did look a bit unusual with his shirt untucked and Willa's leg up on the rail. But they didn't look much more outlandish than some of the other couples who were standing close together in dark corners.

Even standing still, Clint could feel the spot between Willa's legs getting wetter. Just to tantalize her further, he shifted so that he plunged as far into her as he could. Willa responded with a gasp and arched her back, grabbing hold of the edge of the bar with both hands. She pulled herself together a moment later and looked at him hungrily.

"I can't take this anymore," she said. "Either finish what you started or take me somewhere so I can cut loose."

Laughing, Clint said, "You mean this isn't cutting loose? I might not survive if you cut all the way loose."

"Maybe. But aren't you aching to find out?" When she asked that question, Willa tightened the muscles between her legs, clenching around Clint enticingly.

"Let's head for that room you saw," he said. "But first, we need to clean ourselves up a bit."

With a few expert hand movements, Willa had their clothes pulled back on and fastened in a matter of seconds. As soon as they were somewhat decent, Clint took her by the hand and walked quickly toward the door at the back of the room. It stuck a bit, but one good shove got them both through and into a dimly lit space filled mostly by shelves and a large desk.

"This looks like the owner's office," Willa said breathlessly. "Maybe we should—"

But Clint cut her off by taking hold of her beneath both arms, lifting her up, and setting her down on the edge of the desk. His hands went immediately to the buttons on her shirt, pulling them apart as he all but tore the clothing from her body. She wore a thin cotton camisole that clung to her breasts, accentuating the large, rigid nipples.

The summer heat, combined with the heat they'd been generating on their own, had covered their bodies with a film of sweat. On Willa's flesh, it looked more like a dewy sheen that caused the flimsy material of her camisole to stick to her body in a way that made Clint want to slowly peel it off.

"You're right. This is Charlie's office," Clint said, reaching behind himself to lock the door. "But he's busy right now and won't mind if we borrow it."

Willa wore a smile that went from ear to ear. Her eyes glittered with a mischievous fire, and she licked her lips in anticipation. "He's the sheriff, you know. You sure he won't mind if . . ."

"He won't mind," Clint said, sliding his hands under her camisole and cupping her firm, rounded breasts. "Besides, he owes me a favor. And I owe you something else."

FOURTEEN

By the time Grayson had made his way across town and was within a block of the savings and loan, he'd done a fairly good job of convincing himself that he wasn't about to get himself killed. Thoughts like that always flashed through his mind, even when he was just quelling some small-time dispute in his own saloon.

Hell, plenty of lawmen better than him had been killed by a drunk's lucky shot. Even Bat Masterson's brother had been taken down by a similar piece of bad luck. At least, that's what Grayson had heard from one of the drunks who practically lived in The Rusty Nail.

But Grayson tried not to dwell on such things. Being sheriff had plenty of advantages and relatively few drawbacks. Coverdale wasn't a violent town, and most of its lawmen retired due to old age or crossing the wrong politician. Besides, he'd kept his eyes open for those robbers the nervous man had spotted, and had yet to see a single one.

In fact, he was even starting to walk a little taller as he got right across the street from the bank and propped his hands on his hips. Some of the color had come back into his face, and he finally took an easy breath when he saw that there was nothing stirring as far as he could see.

There was nobody in the street.

No one was entering or leaving through the front door.

The shades were drawn, making the entire building look more like a photograph than something he could actually walk up and touch.

Grayson went over those things in his head one more time. All the facts remained the same, but they didn't add up quite as well as when he'd first done the math.

"Oh, hell," he muttered when he saw that the shade had been pulled tightly over the pane of glass set in the front door.

At that moment, the edge of one of the window shades bent ever so slightly. As soon as Grayson looked toward it, the shade snapped back in place and the bank was picture-still once again.

"Oh . . . hell."

As he always did when he got this nervous, Grayson let his hand drop toward the gun at his side. The last man in town to serve as sheriff warned him about doing things like that, but Grayson hadn't concerned himself too much about what that other lawman said. He'd been too concerned with figuring how much his new position could benefit his business. He wished that he'd listened more carefully to all the advice that had been thrown in his direction.

The window whose shade had just been peeled back suddenly shattered outward as though it had been squeezed too tightly in its frame. Large shards of glass hung balanced in place for a split second as smaller razor-sharp bits flew outward.

Grayson had just gotten a glimpse of something dark smashing through the window when the pane beside that first one exploded in a similar manner. Grabbing hold of his gun, he doubled over and spun away from the bank as the air came alive with bursts of gunfire and the hiss of flying lead.

Footsteps came rushing toward him from all sides, the sound assaulting Grayson almost as much as the shots that rang through the air. He had yet to clear leather when he craned his neck to look toward the approaching steps. His eyes turned into saucers when he caught sight of who was coming straight for him.

"Mark!" Grayson shouted. "Thank the Lord it's you!"

The deputy had half a dozen others with him, including Eldon Masters. Two more came from the opposite direction, and all of them converged on the boardwalk across from the bank. All of the deputies except for one ducked behind whatever cover they could find. Mark rushed straight for Grayson, grabbed the lapel of his coat, and threw him behind a watering trough.

Although a bit of anger flashed reflexively in Grayson's eyes, it dissipated less than a second later. He was more happy to be out of the line of fire than he was angry at having been pitched by a deputy.

"How many are there?" Mark asked as he drew his gun and ducked behind the trough next to Grayson.

"I . . . I don't know."

"How long have they been in there?"

"I don't . . ." After taking a moment to collect himself, Grayson took his pistol from its holster, held the cool metal against his cheek, and nodded sharply. "All right," he said with renewed strength in his voice. "That man said there were at least seven of them, right?"

"Damn straight," came a familiar voice from the sheriff's left.

Not too far away, his back pressed against the back of a wooden post, was Eldon Masters. Now that he had a gun in his hand and was dodging bullets, he seemed to have shed at least ten years. His eyes were more alert. His posture was straighter, and there was more color in his skin. Grayson hated to think what he himself looked like just then.

The rest of the deputies had taken up positions behind anything solid. Some were behind other support posts, others were crouched behind barrels, and the rest had gathered around a wagon parked in the street.

Grayson looked around and counted all of the heads he could see. True to his word, Mark had brought all the deputies who had been requested. Besides that, there was the anxious bounty hunter looking to him for orders as well. Of course, even a sheriff still wet behind the ears knew better than to trust a bounty hunter.

"Mark, you take a few men and head around back," Grayson said in a surprisingly steady voice. "The rest of you come with me. We'll either flush them out the back or take them on."

Judging by the looks in the deputies' eyes, every one of them seemed happy with that plan.

"What about me?" Eldon asked.

Grayson looked at him. "You'll stay with me, where I can keep an eye on you. Let's move out."

FIFTEEN

Willa squirmed on the edge of the desk as Clint's hands worked their way down her waist and hips. With a swing of her feet, she kicked her jeans off and tossed them into a pile in front of the office door. She was all smiles and didn't take her eyes off Clint for a second.

"Your turn," she said, dropping her stare toward Clint's unfastened jeans. "And be quick about it."

Clint ripped his feet out of his jeans, then turned his attention back to Willa. For a second, they both stood there, grinning. It might have been because of the forbidden thrill they were sharing—what they were doing plus where they were doing it. Then again, it could also have been their own disheveled appearances that made them take a second to enjoy it.

The moment passed quickly, however, as they cast their eyes downward and saw one another's naked bodies peeking out from beneath layers of rumpled clothing. Willa's shirt was pulled apart and her camisole had been moved up her torso, exposing the bottom half of her breasts. The soft swell of her flesh hung down invitingly while her hard nipples remained trapped behind the flimsy material.

Clint stepped closer so she could unbutton his shirt, allowing her hands to roam over his chest and scrape her fingernails along his flesh. She knew just where to touch him and exactly how long to stay in each spot. The moment he started to enjoy the feel of her hands too much, they moved along, keeping the spark of contact alive.

Both of them were naked from the waist down. Willa's shirttails hung down across her lap, parting at the middle to expose the thatch of hair between her legs and the thin, pink lips within it. Her moisture glistened in the light of the room's lanterns. It felt warm and inviting as Clint reached down to guide the tip of his cock into her waiting vagina.

Spreading her legs even farther, Willa took him inside of her with a satisfied moan that filled the entire room. Clint let out a sigh as well, burying himself deeply inside her. After all of the buildup they'd been putting each other through over the last several minutes, the sensation of finally getting to that point wasn't as good as they thought it would be.

It was better.

Willa locked her hands behind Clint's neck and stared deeply into his eyes. She opened her mouth without saying a word, licking her lips and squirming from side to side as Clint started pumping in and out.

Clint let his hands rest upon Willa's legs, stroking her smoothly muscled contours as he thrust his hips back and forth. When he grabbed hold of her hips and slammed into her even harder, Clint felt every muscle in her lower body tense.

Leaning back just enough to maneuver, Willa peeled her shirt and camisole off and tossed them over Clint's shoulder toward her growing stack of clothes. She then moved her arms behind her and leaned back until she was lying almost completely on the desktop. She groaned softly and wrapped her legs around Clint, arching her back as the first glimmerings of an orgasm built up inside of her.

Clint drank in the sight of her lying in front of him. Her upper body was covered in a fine sheen of sweat, making her flesh glisten as her stomach tensed and her breasts swayed to his thrusting rhythm. He reached out to touch her breast, and the instant his hand got close, she reached up and grabbed hold of it, pressing it tightly against her body.

"God, that feels so good," she groaned. "Keep fucking me just like that."

She spoke without a care as to how she sounded, her voice hard and insistent. The more Willa grunted, the more Clint wanted to hear more. Whereas most women bit down on their lips or stifled the noises they wanted to make during sex, Willa let everything come out. Not only did she groan loudly, but she told Clint where to touch her and for how long.

Most women pleaded for more with a look in their eyes or a whisper, but not Willa. She ordered him to go right where she wanted him.

"Touch me here," she said while guiding his hand to a spot just above her clitoris. "Now fuck me harder."

Clint did as he was told, and felt himself grow harder with every word that came from her mouth. Before she could say anything else, however, he reached down and cupped her buttocks with both hands. He then lifted her off the table and held her against him with his cock still buried between her legs.

Looking surprised and excited, Willa grabbed onto him and pushed up with her arms and legs, easing her pussy up along his shaft before dropping herself back down again. She got more excited when Clint began laying down the law.

"Stand up," he said.

Reluctantly, Willa lowered her feet to the ground and let him drop out of her.

Clint put his hands on her hips while her hands were drawn to his rigid column of flesh, glistening with her moisture.

Doing his best not to react too much to the sensation of her hands stroking his cock, he said, "Now turn around."

She did just that, displaying the magnificent curve of her plump backside.

Without another word, Clint ran his hand over the base of her spine, savoring the feel of her body as she swayed back and forth, breathing heavily in anticipation of what was coming next. His rigid penis fit perfectly between her thighs, sliding inside of her as she let out a prolonged moan.

Clint drove all the way inside of her until his hips were pushing against her buttocks. He then reached forward and took a handful of hair, pulling back just enough to lift Willa's head. When her face came up, she was smiling broadly, gritting her teeth, and clenching her eyes shut.

It was a moment when the rest of the world simply faded away. All Clint could feel was his body being enveloped by hers, the smooth slickness of her skin, and the impact of one body against another as he pounded into her again and again.

SIXTEEN

When Sheriff Grayson looked around the trough, he felt like he was looking at the savings and loan for the first time in his life. The streets around it were still empty and clean—a stark contrast to the shattered glass filling the window frames like jagged teeth and the shades that were filled with blackened bullet holes.

The shots had stopped for the moment, and the smoke-filled air was still. Grayson's heart thumped in his chest and his breath came in ragged bursts. He had to look down to make sure he was still holding his gun—his hands seemed to have gone numb some time ago. The pistol was still there.

Unfortunately . . . so was he.

"All right," he said to his deputies. "You men see if you can get around the back. They might be trying to get out of there." Looking to Mark, he asked, "Isn't that so?"

"Yeah, Sheriff. You're doing fine."

"Then go on."

That was all the deputies needed to hear before the assigned group took off at a run toward the side of the bank building. The men staying behind for the moment emerged from their cover at the same time to unleash another wave of gunfire. What little remained of the front windows was chipped away by flying lead, and the frames themselves were chewed to bits.

For the first couple of seconds, there was no response from inside the savings and loan. Grayson's stomach clenched with the fear that he'd wasted too much time and allowed the robbers to escape. His mind raced with images of armed men running through the streets, shooting anyone who might stand between themselves and a quick way out of town.

At first, when he saw movement at some of the windows and heard the crackle of gunfire, Grayson was actually relieved. That feeling lasted for less than a second as the fight gathered its second wind.

"Cover them!" Grayson shouted. "Mark and the rest are almost there."

The deputies did what they could, hiding behind the limited cover, and maintained their fire for another couple of seconds. It seemed to take forever, but eventually the group of deputies made it across the street and around the savings and loan building. Once they disappeared from view, they were on their own.

Grayson couldn't allow himself to think about them, however. There was plenty more work that needed to be done.

"The rest of you . . . come with me." And with that, Grayson swallowed the knot that was forming in the back of his throat, raised his gun, and moved out from behind the trough.

Grayson made it a few steps before the shots coming from the bank doubled . . . then tripled. More shots went off, but those came from the deputies who had fallen into step behind and around their sheriff. Eldon Masters was running with the charge as well, firing shots into the bank and hollering as he saw one of his bullets set off a spray of blood behind one of the shades.

There wasn't much space to cover before the lawmen were close enough to kick down the bank's front door. Grayson's entire body was charged with adrenaline as he lifted his foot and slammed his boot into the door. Wood splintered and nearly flew inward with the blow. The only thing holding the door in place was the metal latches that had been dropped into their settings within the frame.

As soon as Grayson stepped back for another kick, two of his deputies rushed forward and slammed their shoulders into the door. The impact shook them both all the way down to their bones. The door cracked, but still didn't give.

Grayson looked over to one of the deputies who'd just battered the door. "Hit it again!" he ordered.

The deputy was already starting to lunge forward when a muffled shot filled the air. Grayson heard a solid *thump* and then saw the deputy's eyes roll up into his head. When the other man dropped, the sheriff saw a bearded figure leaning out one of the windows, his gun still smoking in his fist.

Overcome by instinct, Grayson lifted his pistol and pulled the trigger. It was one of the few times he'd actually fired the weapon, but he managed to put his bullet into the bearded man's chest. Grayson knew he would remember the look on that one's face for the rest of his days. Even with that image in mind, his finger pulled the trigger again, sending another round into the killer.

The rest of the deputies followed suit, hitting the robber so many times that by the time he dropped out of the window, the front of his upper body and skull resembled a pile of chewed meat.

More shots came out of the bank, some of which tore through arms and legs of the lawmen. Wise move or not,

Grayson had already committed himself to this frontal assault, and threw his own body against the door. This time, the door was hanging by a few weakened bits of metal, and slammed inward beneath the sheriff's weight.

Grayson fell forward onto his face and into the bank, allowing the rest of the deputies to come surging in from behind him. The interior of the bank smelled like gunpowder, burned wood, and rusty metal. That last smell soaked into Grayson's mind. Within seconds, he knew the scent was blood.

The sheriff got to his feet as a burning pain shot through his left side. One hand went down to cover the spot that seemed to be the source of the nearly blinding pain while the other lifted his pistol and returned fire toward the first unfamiliar face he saw. His eyes went straight to a lanky man with a bandanna hanging over half his face who was staring straight back at him.

The two men looked at one another for no more than half a second. The robber's bandanna wasn't much of a mask. It was merely bunched up around his neck in a way that covered him partially. Because of that, Grayson could see the smile on the man's face and the murderous glint in his eyes as he stared down the barrel of his gun.

Just as Grayson was about to pull his own trigger, the floor next to him shook as a body hit the floor. A shotgun blast thundered through the air like cannon fire, deflecting Grayson's hand enough to send his shot over the robber's head.

The man wearing the bandanna smirked even wider and fired off a shot that punched through Grayson's ribs. His eyes glimmered like a wild animal that had just sunk its fangs into a fresh kill.

Grayson pulled his trigger again, but the hammer of his pistol slapped against a spent round. The metallic clang echoed louder in his ears than any shotgun blast, and he knew that the next thing he heard would be the round that took his life.

Suddenly, the robber's eyes darted away from Grayson and to something the sheriff couldn't see. His hand froze with his finger a hair's width away from pulling his trigger.

"What are you . . . ?" was all the robber could say before his chest exploded with a blast of smoke and blood. His face was a mask of surprise, but only for another second. After that, a second bullet punched through the middle of his skull.

A figure loomed over Grayson and kept moving until it stepped around in front of him. "You all right, Sheriff?" Eldon asked as he knelt down.

"Yeah," Grayson croaked. "Let's clean this mess up."

SEVENTEEN

Clint came out of Grayson's saloon office, hitching his pants up and trying not to smile too widely. Willa was still in the office, straightening up a few odds and ends, mainly trying not to look like she'd been doing what she'd been doing.

Although they'd both been making plenty of noise, the general bustle of the busy saloon would have been more than enough to mask whatever sounds made it through Grayson's door. Besides, the way he was feeling just then, Clint didn't much care what other people might have heard.

He went up to the bar and slapped his hand on the polished surface. The bartender looked up and immediately smiled knowingly as he walked over to where Clint was standing.

"Work up a thirst?" the barkeep asked.

"Just get me a beer."

The man behind the bar smirked again and went about fetching a mug. He could tell that Clint was in fairly good spirits at the moment, but he could also tell that he should watch his step where any off-color ribbing might be concerned. Deciding to play it safe, the barkeep filled a mug from the tap and set it down in front of Clint without any further comment.

Clint took the mug and put a dent in its contents with one sip. When he set it down again, he saw that the barkeep was still standing there looking at him. "Yes," Clint finally said, "I worked up one hell of a thirst."

At that moment, the door behind him opened and Willa came out. She was doing a good job of keeping up her appearances despite the fact that her shirt was rumpled and the buttons were mismatched to the holes. Coming up to the bar, she picked a spot next to Clint and leaned with her elbows on the edge.

"You pick a hell of a time to get reserved," Clint said from the corner of his mouth.

The bartender stifled a chuckle and walked away. Clint couldn't help but laugh as well, and Willa joined in a second later.

Above the sound of voices and the rumble of chairs scraping against the floor, there came a clattering bang as both of the front doors were tossed open with enough force to slam against the wall. Many of the conversations stopped abruptly, and Clint and Willa's laughter was cut short.

"The bank's being robbed!" shouted the young boy who'd burst through the front door.

Clint pushed away from the bar so quickly that he nearly flew back a foot or two. Before he knew what he was doing, he'd already moved through the crowd until he was close enough to get a look at who'd come inside to make that announcement. Several people were already reacting to what had been said, making it that much harder for Clint to make out anything else.

The kid looked to be no more than nine or ten years old. Clint could just see the top of a rapidly moving head before the bat-wing doors flapped and the kid was gone. Clint kept moving through the people. The kid's words had stirred up some excitement, sending ripples through the people like a pebble dropped into a pond.

As Clint emerged from the saloon, others came out with him. Most of them spilled out onto the street, looking around as though they were hoping to hear gunfire or get a look at someone running down a nearby street.

Clint wasn't completely familiar with the layout of the newly grown Coverdale, so he wasn't about to waste his time when he didn't spot the bank in question right away. Instead, he was looking for something else entirely . . . and it appeared to be running down the boardwalk on the way to deliver the news to the next door that would open.

Sprinting toward the kid at full speed, Clint reached him in a couple of long strides and held on to both shoulders. Trying to keep from scaring the youngster, he asked, "What did you say is happening?"

The kid was actually a little girl. She wore dusty pants and a dirty shirt that made her look like she had been running from place to place all day. Her face was smudged with grit and dust that was swirling in the air like a thin mist.

"The bank," she said quickly, "it's being robbed!" Once she got back on that track, the excitement of what she was saying outweighed the startle Clint had given her. "The sheriff and a bunch of men are down there right now. I saw it all start, so I need to find my pa."

"Where's the bank?"

"Straight down there," the little girl said.

Even as he turned to look where the child was pointing, Clint could hear gunshots in the distance. "Get on out of here," he said, swatting the kid lightly on the behind to get her going. "And don't even think about going near that bank until this is over."

"Yessir." And with that, the kid scurried off until she reached the cathouse two doors down from The Rusty Nail. Once there, she threw open the door and stuck her head inside, screaming, "The bank's being robbed!"

Clint was already on his way down the street. With the sun all the way down, it was easier to make out where he was going. Darkness was kinder to the eyes than the glaring rays of the setting sun.

"Where you going?" Willa asked as she ran to catch up with him.

"To the bank. The sheriff's a friend of mine." Thinking back to the last time he'd caught sight of Charlie, Clint could still see the troubled look on Charlie's face. "Dammit! Why didn't he ask for my help?"

"Because he probably didn't know what he was getting into. Besides, you're not a deputy. We couldn't even hear the shots being fired inside that saloon." When Clint turned to look at her, Willa quickly added, "Anywhere in that saloon."

Clint had broken into a run, headed toward the crackle of gunfire and the bustle of voices.

"What are you doing?" Willa asked, sprinting to keep up.

"I'm going to help Charlie."

"Not without me, you're not!"

EIGHTEEN

In the short time it took Clint and Willa to cover the distance between The Rusty Nail and Coverdale's savings and loan building, the sky seemed to have gotten black as pitch. The last rays of the sun had faded a while ago, but true night had held off until they arrived. Once the summer sky finally revealed the stars, the fight at the bank was getting down to its bare bones.

Clint spotted the bodies scattered on the street at and near the bank. Some of them wore a badge on their chest, and others had their face covered by a bandanna or a scarf. Still others were indistinguishable. They didn't look like lawmen or bandits. They just looked dead.

"Why are you still here?" Clint asked Willa as he approached the bank, his Colt in hand.

When he looked over at her, he saw that she was brandishing a weapon of her own. The .45 that he'd seen earlier was now clutched in her hand.

"I'm not leaving you just because you said so. Besides . . . I can help if you'll just give me a chance."

"I don't have time to debate this. Just stick close to me and try not to get hurt."

Without further delay, Clint jumped up the stairs leading to the front entrance and rushed inside, stepping over the door, which had already been knocked off its hinges. From what he could see, the fight was at a standstill. Men were still shooting freely at one another, but both sides had found cover and were firmly entrenched.

As Clint and Willa burst into the building, some of the fire was turned in their direction. Luckily, Clint spotted a familiar face and headed toward the group who had barricaded themselves behind a row of overturned tables and a solid oak desk.

Across the room, one of the bandits popped his head out from behind the counter that spanned the back of the room. Although the cages had been knocked out of the tellers' windows, the counter was solid wood, a perfect shield for the thieves.

The bandit who looked out squeezed off a shot at Clint, prompting a few more to do the same. As Clint threw himself behind the lawmen's barricade, the Colt barked twice in quick succession. One round dug a splintered trench over the top of the counter, and the second dug a messy hole through the first bandit's forehead.

Two of the four deputies crouched behind the barricade leveled their weapons at Clint and Willa. Even though one of the bandits had just been picked off, the lawmen didn't seem to be in the mood for new arrivals.

One of the deputies glared at Clint, snarling, "Who the hell are—"

Mark cut him off with a hand on his shoulder. "It's all right. The sheriff says he knows this one."

At that moment, Clint spotted Charlie huddled at the other end of the barricade. The blood on the sheriff's clothes was plain to see. So was the fact that the lawman was doing everything in his power to keep from keeling over from the pain of his wounds. "Charlie, what did you get yourself into?"

"It's a bit of a scrape all right," Grayson said in a strained voice. "Kind of took me by surprise."

"Those damn killers would've been long gone with the money by now if Sheriff Grayson hadn't charged in here," Mark said, rushing to his defense.

Clint nodded. "Looks like you lost a lot of men."

"A few," Mark conceded. "But they lost more. Far as we can tell, just the leader and one or two others are left."

"How many total?"

"Less than a dozen."

Charlie hacked up a breath and gathered his strength. "Seven. There was seven at first. Some more came riding in later."

Mark was helping the sheriff keep his balance. "That's right. I don't know for sure how many more came in, but they must've been waiting for the rest. They rode in not too long after the shooting started. We've got some men positioned out back. We don't know how many of them are still left, though. Or . . . if there's *any* of them left."

Turning his attention to the bandits who were still firing occasional shots toward the barricade, Clint took a careful look at the lay of the land. "There must be some of them left. Otherwise, these fellas here would have been long gone already."

"I'll tell you one thing," Willa said. "If we don't do something, those men *will* be long gone. They're working their way toward the window."

"What?" Mark said.

Willa pointed toward the wall. "When we came in, the shots were coming from the middle of that counter. Now they're coming from closer to the wall. A couple more feet and they can make a break for it."

Clint plucked a bullet from his gun belt and quickly

snapped it into the Colt's cylinder to replace the one he had fired. "That's not going to happen," he said.

Grayson gathered his legs beneath him like a bobcat about to spring. The look in his eyes was like nothing Clint had seen in the man before. There was no fear or hesitation. All of that was replaced by a grim resolve to get a job done. "You men get ready. We came this far . . . and we're not letting those bastards out of here. We make one more move now."

The deputies prepared themselves without question, like infantrymen gathering behind their general. Even Clint found himself wanting to obey Charlie's command.

Sensing what was about to happen, the bandits intensified their fire. Clint could tell there weren't too many of them, but they had the advantage of better cover. Of course, the lawmen had an advantage now as well. They had The Gunsmith on their side.

NINETEEN

As soon as Grayson stood up and bolted from around the barricade, the rest of what happened became a blur in Clint's mind. He charged from around the piled-up tables and desk with bullets whipping by his head. He took shots whenever he could, and managed to force the bandits to keep their heads down.

One thing Clint knew for sure was that Willa stayed right next to him. Bullets from her .45 roared through the air, punching holes into the counter as she, Clint, and the lawmen made their final strike.

The charge was only about three seconds long and covered twenty feet, but it had all the elements of a battlefield maneuver. The bullets coming at them were real, and the specter of death was looking down on them.

Clint made it to the counter, then placed the palm of one hand on top of it so he could vault over. As he was hoisting himself up and over, he saw an angry, dirty face glaring up at him from behind a pair of smoking pistols. Clint managed to twist his body as he was coming down, angling himself so that he could kick out with one foot while landing on the other. His toe landed on the side of one of the bandit's guns, knocking it toward the other gun as they both went off.

The bandit's face disappeared behind a cloud of smoke as his weapons fired. Just as Clint got his second foot beneath him, the bandit aimed with the hand that hadn't been kicked and tensed his finger around the trigger.

Clint reacted instinctively, pointing his Colt like his finger and squeezing the trigger. The modified pistol sent a single round through the air, drilling the bandit squarely between the eyes as his gun went off.

A round hissed through the air to Clint's left, scraping along his side and leaving a nasty scratch in its wake. The man who fired it slumped backward, spilling the contents of his head onto the floor.

"Clint, look out!" Willa shouted.

By the time Clint responded, he saw another bandit taking aim at him with a shotgun. Before Clint got his Colt in position to fire, two shots went off close by. One came from behind him as Willa blew a hole in the bandit's chest with her .45. The other came from behind the shotgunner, causing him to jerk like a puppet being pulled on strings.

When that bandit dropped, Clint could find no others. All that was left behind the counter was himself, Willa and the deputy who'd put the bullet through the shotgunner's back. Clint instantly looked around for Charlie, but couldn't find any trace of his friend. And Grayson's body wasn't among the fresh ones on the floor.

"That way!" Willa said as she leaped over the shotgunner's corpse. "They've got to be that way."

She was headed for a door farther behind the counter. There was a short hallway leading to either offices or the vault. But what caught everyone's attention was a door that swung open, revealing a glimpse of the outside.

"Wait!" Clint said as he bolted toward the back door.

But Willa was already there, and she didn't seem the least bit inclined to listen to what Clint was saying.

Shots were coming from outside, and in a matter of moments, Clint was at the door. It opened into a small courtyard that was just big enough to hold a couple horses and maybe a small wagon. It emptied into a wide alleyway, which was where most of the activity was taking place.

Clint took a quick count and spotted half a dozen people scattered in the courtyard. There was nowhere to hide, so the combatants were forced to throw themselves into the line of fire.

It looked like two of the men were trying to get into the alley. The men trying to stop them wore badges, so Clint knew those two had to be all that was left of the bandits. Both of them had their guns out and were firing at all of the deputies around them; their eyes were burning with a fire kindled by desperate rage.

"Put . . . your guns down!" Grayson shouted. His voice was strained, hampered by the pain that continually assaulted his body.

Clint could see the bloodstains on Charlie's clothes getting darker. He also could see a man without a badge coming up on Charlie's right, advancing toward the alley.

Mark stepped forward when the badgeless man started to advance. "Eldon, no!"

One of the bandits heading toward the alley caught sight of Eldon. His eyes went wide, and he stopped dead in his tracks. "What are you doing her—"

The bandit's words were cut off as Eldon's hand flashed up and his gun spat out smoke and sparks. He'd been gripping a rifle in both hands, his knuckles turning white with the effort. He took his shot a split second after Eldon pulled his trigger. The rifle bullet hissed past its target, but Eldon's round pounded straight into the bandit's face, drilling all the way through and flying out the other side.

Before anyone could blink, Eldon's gun flashed again, turning the bandit's head into bloody pulp.

"Best stay right where you are," Eldon said to the last remaining gunman.

The deputies lined up behind Eldon. Willa was moving to stand beside the bounty hunter, but Clint held her back. She started to protest, but held her tongue when she saw the look in Clint's eyes. Instead, she let him walk slowly toward the bandit.

"It's over," Clint said, covering the last bandit with his Colt. "Drop your gun."

"Stand aside," one of the deputies said.

Clint looked at the man who'd spoken, making sure to keep the bandit in sight as well. "Someone come take this man to jail."

"Oh, we're taking him all right," the deputy said as he levered a fresh round into his shotgun. "But it won't be to jail. Him and his men killed a lot of our friends here tonight. For that . . . we're taking him straight to hell."

"Maybe you should check with the sheriff before you make a call like that," Clint said. "Charlie . . . what do you think?"

But Charlie Grayson didn't answer. He was too busy dying.

TWENTY

Willa moved like a cat as she stepped forward and snatched the gun from the last bandit's hand. He offered no resistance—several deputies were about ready to blow his head off. As soon as he was disarmed, the outlaw lowered himself to one knee and folded his hands over his head.

"Oh, you're used to this, aren't ya?" Willa said as she reached behind her and pulled a set of handcuffs from a pouch at the small of her back.

Clint saw that the killer was secured before he holstered his Colt and rushed to Charlie's side. When he got there, Charlie was gasping for air and blood was pouring out of him like a crimson river.

"Charlie?" Clint said as he knelt down and lifted the sheriff's head off the ground. "Can you hear me, Charlie?"

Mark was there as well, standing over Sheriff Grayson's body like he was guarding it from the Grim Reaper. One of the deputies aimed his gun at the cuffed outlaw and took an occasional glance down at the fallen sheriff. "How bad is it? He's going to be all right, isn't he?"

Clint was no doctor, but he knew light wounds from bad ones. Although Charlie hadn't been hit in the heart or the head, he'd sustained enough smaller wounds for them to add up to something terrible. Also, it looked as though that last stray rifle shot might have clipped one of his lungs.

When Charlie opened his mouth to speak, pink foam gurgled in his throat and spilled out the corner of his mouth. It looked like a dirty version of soda bubbles or the stuff floating at the top of a pond. Coming from Charlie's mouth like that, Clint knew it couldn't be good.

"Did . . . did we get them?" Charlie croaked.

Clint nodded, although he doubted Charlie could see him. "Yeah. We got them."

". . . Th . . . they're probably wanted . . . men."

"Probably."

"I think . . . I got shot, Clint. Did I get shot?"

"Afraid so, buddy," Clint said without allowing his voice to waver. "But we'll get you taken care of."

Standing by the bodies of the bandits who had fallen in the courtyard and near the alley, Eldon took a closer look at the one with the rifle.

The cuffs were secured around the last bandit's wrists, and he was tossed up against a wall. Some of the other deputies still had their guns on him. They wanted to shoot him so badly that their blood lust could almost be smelled on the air, an acrid scent.

"I . . . messed . . . up," Charlie said. "I should've . . . never . . . been sheriff."

"Don't say that. You did a good job. These men would have gotten away if it wasn't for you."

"Thanks, Clint . . . but I know . . . better."

"All you know is that you're hurting. We'll get you fixed up, Charlie. I promise you that."

Charlie shook his head. He tried to speak, but by now

the foam was mixed with blood and his words were a pained croak.

Looking down at the sheriff, Mark shook his head and gripped his weapon a little tighter. "Jesus Christ, they killed him."

The deputies who had gathered around the sheriff stared down at Charlie as though they couldn't quite believe what they were seeing. The rest were lined up like a firing squad, just waiting for the command to execute the cuffed prisoner.

All that prevented them from carrying out their sentence was an obstruction positioned between them and their target.

"Get out of the way, ma'am."

Clint heard that, and looked up to see what was going on. Willa was standing in front of the outlaw with her arms placed defiantly on her hips. She wasn't making a move to draw her gun.

"Willa, what are you doing?" Clint asked.

"I won't let them kill him," she said. By the tone in her voice, she was dead serious, and no number of guns pointed at her was going to change her mind.

Looking around, Clint saw that the only man who wasn't either at Charlie's side or pointing a gun at Willa was Eldon. He was standing over the freshest corpse, staring down at it as though expecting it to get up and do a dance.

"I need everyone's help here," Clint said after summing up the situation as best he could. "The sheriff needs to get to a doctor, and he doesn't have much time to get there. All of you men help me with him." Focusing his voice on the men who were lined up in front of Willa and the prisoner, he added, "All of you."

"Don't bother them . . . with that," Charlie wheezed. He was spitting up the foamy blood, but the words were coming a little easier now. "It's too late for me . . . I told you."

"Don't say that. If you want to make it through this, you're going to have to believe you can. You've got to pull up the strength to make it, Charlie!"

Even as he said that, Clint was believing it less and less. His hands were underneath Charlie's head and torso, supporting his weight as he tried to get him to move. The blood seeping through his fingers was so thick that it felt like a sticky paste was sealing them together.

"Somebody help me!" Clint yelled.

That snapped the rest of the deputies out of wanting to execute the last outlaw like a cold bucket of water poured down their backs. They turned away from the prisoner and lowered their weapons, rushing over to Clint so they could help get Charlie up and on his feet.

Charlie let out a grating breath as he was lifted up and held between Clint and Mark. When his head slumped forward, his mouth drooped open and let out a thick stream of the pink, foamy blood. Every breath was hard and ragged, yet somehow he never got any air.

Clint was no doctor, but even he figured that the last bullet had indeed clipped one of Charlie's lungs. At that moment, as if to verify what he was thinking, the wound in Charlie's chest made a wet sucking noise that caused a knot to form in the bottom of Clint's stomach.

With the deputies' help, Clint was able to get Charlie moving. One of the lawmen took the lead because Clint didn't know where the doctor's office was. The weight of his friend was getting heavier with every step. The sound coming from Charlie's chest was getting even louder than the attempts at breathing which came from his mouth.

Before they left the courtyard, Clint saw that Willa was tending to the prisoner. She shoved him roughly in front of her, grabbing hold of the chain that held his wrists together. Eldon was still looking down at the rifleman's body.

"You, there," Clint said to him, "come with us. We may need your help if Sheriff Grayson can't move his legs."

"He's finished," Eldon said.

"Shut the hell up. Come over here and help us!"

As though he just realized the rest of the world was there, Eldon looked toward Clint and the rest. He fell into step with the group while his eyes kept darting back to that one particular corpse.

"Put me down," Charlie wheezed.

Clint shook his head and kept walking slowly. "We're not there yet. Just a little farther."

"Thanks for everything, Clint. I'm sorry . . . I wasn't a . . . better. . . ."

Suddenly, Charlie's body went limp. He didn't feel the way a man does when he goes unconscious. Clint had dragged his fair share of unconscious men from one point to another, so he knew how that felt. Even unconscious men still felt like men. Their bodies still felt like bodies.

In the space of that instant, Charlie's body took on a weight that was different than if he'd just passed out. None of his muscles were helping to support him . . . not even subconsciously. His instinct to hold on for support sputtered out, and he sagged like something that had been stitched together out of wet rags and slabs of beef.

"Come on, Charlie!" Clint yelled, even though he knew it wasn't any use. "Just a little farther!"

Suddenly, Clint realized that he was the only one trying to move Charlie. The rest of the men were holding him up, but looking at the sheriff's face with forlorn sadness.

Charlie was gone.

TWENTY-ONE

Charlie was gone.

Everyone knew it.

Clint didn't make a sound as he lowered the body to the ground. Mark was the one to lean forward and close the sheriff's eyes while Clint stared into his face. Once that was done, both of them got to their feet and looked down at Charlie.

Clint had never felt so helpless. All he could do was look up at the stars, ball his fists, and walk away.

He didn't go far. All he wanted to do was take a few steps away until he was no longer choking on the stink of death. Around him, the deputies shuffled on their feet and spoke among themselves. Clint knew they must be feeling worse than he was; since Charlie wasn't the only lawman to fall in the last hour. But if Clint thought about all those others who had been shot, he knew he would just feel worse.

Behind him, he could hear Mark assigning jobs to the rest of the deputies, mostly some type of cleanup detail. But the voices behind him seemed to stay at the same level. In fact, for a group that was supposed to be going different places to do their jobs, nobody seemed to be going anywhere.

Clint pulled himself together and walked back to where everyone was standing. Mark was the one everyone else was looking toward for leadership. As far as what Mark had to say, none of the other men seemed to like that one bit.

"To hell with the rest of those men," one of the deputies snarled. "They're all dead. We know that for damn sure."

Another of the lawmen stepped forward. "Yeah. And that one should be, too!" He pointed toward the prisoner, who was still standing behind Willa.

"Everyone just shut your mouths and listen to me," Mark said. "We have to do what we came here for. Sheriff Grayson would have wanted it that way."

"Sheriff Grayson's dead. And that one over there killed him."

Hearing that, Willa straightened up and took hold of her .45. She kept it in its holster, but looked ready to draw at a moment's notice.

Clint walked over to stand at Mark's side. The look on his face was enough to quiet most of the others. For a minute, Mark didn't seem to know there was someone beside him. But when he turned to see Clint, he squared off without hesitation.

"I don't know who the hell you think you are, but you're not a part of this."

"I was Charlie's friend."

"Well, this is a matter for the law to decide now. Your help is no longer needed."

"Is that so? Then you're just going to have to send a few of these men to remove me, because I'm not going anywhere. After the hit you all took tonight, I doubt you could spare any manpower on something like that."

Mark nodded, and his expression lightened up a bit.

"First things first. We need to make sure we got all of the men trying to rob this place and see if they got away with any money. Also, if there are any more of them about, they'll be desperate to get out of town, and just might hurt someone in the process."

"I agree," Clint said. "I can help look for any that might have gotten away."

"And I can help with that." Willa came forward, still leading the prisoner like an animal by the chain between his wrists. "I'm not a bad tracker."

"Neither am I," Eldon said from outside the group. "But I doubt that any of them got away."

"What makes you say that?" Mark asked.

"Because this here is their leader."

All of the deputies looked toward Eldon. Even Clint stared at him for a moment or two. The closer he examined that one, the less he seemed like an old man and the more he seemed like someone who'd just been chewed up and spit out by the world. That tended to add a few years to a man's face.

Clint walked over to Eldon and looked down at the body that the bounty hunter had been staring at for the last several minutes. The dead man's face, bloody and twisted, didn't strike Clint as familiar. Then again, he didn't make it his business to memorize the faces that were plastered on Wanted posters all across the country.

"Who is he?" Clint asked.

Eldon smiled faintly and shook his head as though looking down on an old friend. "He's someone I've been after for a fair bit of time. His name is Kevin Stohls."

TWENTY-TWO

If anything was going to snap the deputies out of squabbling among themselves, that name seemed to be it. Even though the name didn't register in Clint's mind right away, every one of the lawmen stopped what he was doing and moved over to Eldon.

"Jesus Christ," one of the younger deputies said. "Is that really Kevin Stohls?"

Eldon nodded. "None of these others look familiar, but that one over there"—he pointed toward the man being dragged behind Willa—"he's been riding with him for a good number of years."

Now all of the deputies turned toward Willa. Thinking that she would be in the clear for a little bit thanks to Eldon's distraction, her face fell, and she once again took up her defensive stance.

"That one's name is James Carroll," Eldon said. "He and Stohls were like brothers. They were the only members of the gang who never changed over the years."

Now that he'd heard the name a few more times, Clint was starting to remember stories he'd heard about the Stohls gang. Some of them came from newspapers, but mostly they were passed by word of mouth inside saloons and around card tables. In the world of men who made their living on their reputation, thcse were the places a reputation was made . . . or broken.

Clint stepped away from the body, allowing another of the deputies to get a closer look. He was more interested in Willa at that moment and went over to her.

The man she was holding prisoner was making no attempt to escape. It wasn't that his spirit was broken or that he lacked courage. He just had enough of his wits about him to recognize a bad situation. His life was hanging by a thread. That much was obvious. The only certainty was that he would die in a hail of gunfire if he tried anything right then.

Standing in front of Willa, Clint looked behind her, into the prisoner's eyes. Something about his face did seem familiar, but it wasn't anything that knocked Clint back.

Looking once again at Willa, Clint asked, "You're a bounty hunter, aren't you?"

She nodded. "I never tried to hide that from anyone."

"But you didn't exactly come out and say it, either."

"There was no reason to tip my hand to anyone."

"So you want to keep the reward for that one all to yourself. Is that why you're guarding him like a wolf guarding its young?"

"I'm willing to share the money. But there's more offered if he's alive. It seems a shame to lose out on something like that just because a few cowboys can't keep from getting their hackles up and calling for blood."

The deputies turned to glare at her. This time, Mark looked just as angry as the rest of them.

"He'll be dead enough," Willa assured them. "Him and Stohls weren't strangers to killing lawmen. They did the same down in North Carolina, and the law there's been chomping at the bit to get their hands on these two. Once they hear what happened here tonight, I wouldn't be surprised if they paid for train tickets to ship all of you men down there to watch the hanging."

"How much is the reward?"

That question was on everyone's mind, but Eldon was the one who didn't have any problem asking it.

"Fifty thousand for James, here. Stohls would've fetched sixty if he was alive, but his body's worth thirty."

Eldon let out a low whistle; the deputies stared coldly at Willa. Clint admired them for that. If they started licking their chops at the prospect of getting rich off of this with Charlie's body still lying in plain sight, he might have had to turn his back on the whole thing.

The courtyard was silent for a little bit. All that could be heard for the next couple of seconds was the rustle of the wind and the gentle clinking of the prisoner's chains as he shifted from one foot to another.

Clint stepped closer to Willa, staring into her eyes as though he was peering into her soul. "You're sure this is James Carroll?"

"Yep," she said without hesitation. "Otherwise, I wouldn't have risked my life by standing between him and these deputies."

One thing that Clint could recognize was a liar. He'd had the best of them try to pull things on him, and sometimes he'd been conned. But not once could he remember looking square into someone's eyes, watching them talk, and not spot it when they were flat-out lying to him. His life depended upon that particular skill.

"Fine," he said. "But don't be offended if I check on it myself."

She nodded and returned his gaze. In fact, she held her chin a little higher after that had been said. It seemed as though she saw something in his eyes as well. If she was any kind of bounty hunter, she needed to be a fair judge of men.

Turning to the deputies, Clint looked at each of them in turn. "Sheriff Grayson was a good man. I won't have his memory tarnished by executing someone right here and now. He would have wanted us to do the right thing here."

One of the younger, outspoken deputies started to step forward, but was stopped when Mark grabbed him by the elbow and whispered something in his ear. The deputy's eyes widened a little, and some of the color drained from his face. He turned and spoke in a hushed tone to another deputy. The whispering spread through all of them like wildfire, until every one of them was wearing the same expression on his face.

"So you're Clint Adams?" the younger deputy asked.

Clint nodded.

"Then you really did know the sheriff. Some of us didn't believe him when he said he knew you."

That brought a little smile to Clint's face. It was almost as if he could once again hear Charlie's voice as he told his tall tales inside The Rusty Nail. His smile faded the instant he caught a glimpse of the sheriff's body sprawled on the ground.

"Well, I did know him," Clint said. "And for right now, we should take care of what needs doing. This place needs to be cleaned up and . . . Charlie needs a decent burial. In fact," he added, turning to Willa, "he'll get the best service money can buy and a hell of a party afterward . . . all compliments of our friend in the metal bracelets over there."

The mood among the deputies immediately darkened. "So he's going back to North Carolina?" the younger one asked.

"He is," Clint answered.

"Dead or alive?"

"We want him to face the justice that's coming to him, so he'll be going back alive. That way, the men he and Stohls hurt down in North Carolina will get their justice as well. They've been waiting a long time. I'm sure they've got plenty of things planned before James here sees the end of a noose."

Clint had been turning slowly as he spoke. By the time he said that last part, he was face-to-face with James Carroll. The outlaw's face was set in a grim mask, but Clint could see a lot going on inside his eyes. "You don't like that too much, do you?"

James said nothing.

"You sure don't. I can see the fear inside of you plain as day." Clint spoke in an intense whisper that tore through the bandit like claws through newspaper. "And you're right to be afraid after what happened here, you son of a bitch. It's a long way to North Carolina. A lot can happen from here to there."

"I heard of you," James said. "You won't kill me. Not in cold blood."

"I won't be the only one going with you. And besides . . . there's a whole lot on the road to death. A whole lot of pain . . . and a whole lot more fear. But I don't have to tell you that. You'll find out just as well on your own."

TWENTY-THREE

Grayson's deputies had done a thorough job. Not a trace of any remaining bandits could be found by the men who went looking.

And Mark did a good job of taking over for Charlie. Watching the senior deputy in action, Clint figured that he'd been doing a lot of the work when Charlie was alive. Mark knew how to deal with the others, even in this hard time, and delegated enough tasks to keep bodies busy and minds away from the thirst for revenge.

Clint escorted Willa, a deputy, and James to a cell. He didn't say a word to any of them during the entire time, which made the relatively short walk to the jailhouse seem extraordinarily long. Once the cell door was opened, James stepped inside and sat down with a heavy sigh. He lowered his head and stared at the floor.

The remaining deputies filtered into the small building that housed the sheriff's office one at a time. Clint was surprised at the number of them, especially considering that he'd seen more than a few lying dead or wounded at the savings and loan. He didn't concern himself with that for the moment, however. Clint merely took some comfort knowing that Coverdale wasn't in any danger of being unprotected until another sheriff was found.

Clint then went back to the bank. Seeing it after being away for a little while made the scene look more like a war zone than anything else. Some of the bodies had been gathered up by the undertaker and his assistants, who stacked them in the back of a wagon like firewood.

There weren't as many dead as Clint had thought. Many of them were unconscious from their wounds and several of the deputies were gathering up a couple of bandits who were still breathing and throwing them unceremoniously into a cramped cell.

As if he was overseeing this, Eldon stood in the shadows, haunting the scene like a specter.

"What's the matter?" Clint asked. "I thought you'd be picking through those carcasses and claiming some of them for yourself."

Eldon shook his head and fished a slender cigar out of his shirt pocket. "Nah. These boys hadn't done enough to make them worth the effort."

"True. And you could always dig them up if you found out anything different."

Striking a match against the wall behind him, Eldon touched the flame to the end of his cigar. "You don't like me too much, do you, Adams? What is it . . . something against men in my line of work?"

"Not particularly. Just you."

"And why's that?"

"I don't know yet. There's just something about you that doesn't sit right with me."

"I'll have you know that I did my best to help cover your friend the sheriff's ass. He didn't know too much about what he was doing. That much was certain."

Clint held his tongue for a moment, letting out a controlled breath before saying, "I'm tired, Eldon. Also, I can't say I disagree with you regarding Charlie's law enforcement skills. But do yourself a favor and stop talking before you say something that gives me the strength to knock you on your ass."

The cigar burned brightly as Eldon inhaled slowly. He let the smoke roll around his mouth for a bit before looking up and sending it toward the stars. He glanced at Clint . . . nodded . . . and took another puff.

"Smart move," Clint said. Then he walked away, leaving the bounty hunter to finish his cigar alone.

When he reached the courtyard behind the savings and loan, Clint saw the undertaker standing over Charlie's body. Without saying a word, Clint went over and stood at Charlie's shoulders, and both men lifted him up. They carried him to the undertaker's wagon, where his was the last body to be stacked on the pile.

It was a gruesome end to a terrible night, and Clint wanted nothing more than to get away from it all. There was only one place he wanted to be at that moment, so that was where he headed.

TWENTY-FOUR

The night was still young by saloon standards, and The Rusty Nail was brimming with life. It was a strange but welcome contrast to all the death that had been surrounding Clint that evening.

It felt good to be inside the place. The news of Charlie's death had already circulated through the entire town, so most of the people there could talk about nothing else. Unlike the deputies, however, the folks inside the saloon dwelled on the happier times, swapping funny stories about The Rusty Nail's owner and raising their glasses to him at every opportunity.

Clint was starting to feel a smile coming to his face as he listened to the stories and remembered some of his own. That smile faded a bit when the bat-wing doors swung open and Willa Singer stepped inside.

At that moment Clint realized he was standing at the same spot he and Willa had shared before the shooting had started. He felt more than a little uncomfortable once that realization hit him.

She walked straight up to him, cutting through the crowd as though she knew before she'd walked through the door where to find him. Once at his side, she waved to the barkeep and ordered a pair of whiskey shots. There was an uncomfortable silence until the drinks arrived. After setting both glasses down in front of her, the barkeep left her and Clint alone.

She put the first glass to her lips, tipped it back, and downed the shot in one gulp. Willa set the empty glass down, but kept her fingers wrapped around it. Her eyes were fixed on a point in space between herself and the polished wooden surface.

Looking over to the other glass, Clint said, "I don't drink whiskey."

"Who said that was for you?" And with that, she took the second glass and emptied it even quicker than the first, slapping it down onto the bar.

After a few moments, she turned so that she was leaning against the bar with her hip. Willa then reached out and put a hand on Clint's shoulder. "I know what's bothering you, Clint. It won't do any good to keep it bottled up like this."

"And it didn't do Charlie any good with me in the back room with you while he was getting pumped full of bullets."

She nodded, gritting her teeth. Even though she'd been expecting him to say it, that didn't make the words any easier to hear. "We had no way of knowing what was happening. We couldn't hear the gunshots from here, and nobody would expect you to."

"Why are you talking like you would have helped him, too?" Clint asked, wheeling around to look at her with such intensity that she seemed stricken by his expression. "All you were worried about was your money. . . ." Suddenly, Clint straightened up. "You were in town only for those men, weren't you?"

He waited and watched her. Keeping his eyes fixed on

Willa, he studied every aspect of the woman, which told him more than any words could express.

Working on her instincts, Willa knew she couldn't hide anything from Clint . . . even if she'd wanted to. "I'd heard Stohls was going to be pulling a big job somewhere in the area, and this seemed the most likely target."

"Then why didn't you say anything?"

Willa took hold of one of the empty shot glasses and slammed it down on the bar. "I did," she said. "I told Sheriff Grayson about it when I came to town. I even told him that Stohls might be nearby and could be here any time. You know what he said?"

Clint kept perfectly still. When he spoke, his lips barely parted. "Tell me."

"He told me there wasn't anybody foolish enough to try and steal anything from that bank. Especially since half the town's able-bodied men had signed up to be sheriff's deputies."

Clint shook his head in a way that made Willa think that she would be better off leaving the saloon and not coming back. She stood her ground, however, and watched as he turned to prop both elbows back onto the edge of the bar.

"Dammit," Clint said. "Why the hell did Charlie have to go and run for sheriff? Why couldn't he just stay in this place where he was safe?"

"I don't know. But if it helps any, I'd say you weren't the only one thinking along those lines. Did you get a look at that deputy who glued himself to the sheriff's side?"

"You mean Mark? I saw him, all right. He looked like he didn't know whether he should listen to Charlie or punch him in the face. The funny thing is, I know exactly how he felt."

Clint looked over at Willa for a moment before allowing the anger to drain from his face. Actually, it left his face and a good portion of his body as well. Seeing that she wasn't on his bad side for the time being, Willa moved a little closer to Clint.

"You really shouldn't blame yourself for what happened," she said. "You had no way of knowing what was going on, and I wasn't entirely sure Stohls was coming to this town so soon. Usually, he's a little more careful before taking on a bank like that."

"Yeah, but Charlie shouldn't have gone in there alone like that."

Willa reached out and placed her fingers along the side of Clint's chin, moving his face so that he was looking directly into her eyes. "Like it or not . . . and I get the feeling that plenty of people didn't . . . that man was the town's sheriff. He went in there to do what sheriffs do. Charlie was doing his job, Clint. The man I saw in that bank didn't look like some pug who should have stayed behind a bar. He looked like a true lawman doing his best to stop those killers."

Nodding, Clint said, "He sure did, didn't he?"

Willa motioned for the bartender, and got the man to refill one of her shot glasses with whiskey. Then she raised her glass and said, "Here's to Charlie."

Clint lifted his beer. "To Charlie."

TWENTY-FIVE

Clint woke up early the next morning, as was his habit. It was a little past dawn, but not much, and when he walked down the stairs in the hotel, the smell of breakfast hung heavy in the air. He'd been intending to get straight to business that day, but he was only human, and the scent of fresh bacon and biscuits was more than he could bear.

Willa came down with him. They took their time filling their stomachs, since there didn't seem to be anything else happening in the town.

Once their bellies were full, Clint and Willa headed to the sheriff's office. Even thinking those words brought a sobering chill to Clint's mind. The building next to the jailhouse used to be Charlie's office. Now he had to face the fact that Charlie was dead all over again.

Unfortunately, Clint was all too used to bidding farewell to his friends. It never seemed to get any easier, no matter how many times he went through it.

Clint decided to go to the jailhouse first. He poked his head into the cramped little building and saw two deputies guarding one man. He was even happier that another deputy came up behind him to check on who was looking in on the prisoner.

"You've got security up to snuff, I see."

"Yes, sir, Mister Adams." It was the younger, more outspoken deputy who had walked up behind Clint. "We even managed to round up some volunteers to help fill in for . . . well . . . to help us. Mostly brothers and cousins of ours, but they've been doing good enough."

"What about Eldon?" Willa asked. "I don't suppose he gave up and headed out of town?"

Just then, Eldon stepped around the corner. He looked every bit as rumpled as he had the night before, making it tough to figure out if he'd gotten any sleep or had been leaning against the outside of the jailhouse all night long. "You won't be getting rid of me until we get to North Carolina."

Willa looked at the other bounty hunter as though he ranked somewhere below a tapeworm on her list of favorite things. "What makes you think you'll be coming with us?"

Grinning, Clint asked Willa, "And what makes you think that *you'll* be coming with us?"

"Because if you don't bring me along, I'm afraid you might get yourself hurt."

"Is that a fact? You think I might be in jeopardy from this fella in the chains?"

"No. I think I might have to hurt you if you don't let me see this through to the end."

There was no threat or malice in her voice. It was a simple statement of fact, tinged with a hint of humor. Clint looked into her eyes and knew that it would be a mistake to laugh too hard at that joke.

"Fine," he said. Turning to Eldon, Clint added, "And as for you. . . ."

"As for me, nothing," Eldon said in his scratchy voice. "I'm going, too, and that's the end of it."

Every time he heard him speak, Clint caught something

different about Eldon Masters. This time, apart from the fact that he didn't seem half as old when he talked in his normal voice and stood up straight, Clint saw something subtly menacing in Eldon's manner. It wasn't anything that made Clint feel threatened; it was just an edge he hadn't noticed before.

"What were you doing at that bank robbery?" Clint asked.

The deputy stepped forward to answer the question. "I can vouch for him, Mister Adams. He was right there when it happened, and even helped us when the shooting started."

"The old man's all right," came a voice from outside the main group. Walking up to the jailhouse from the direction of the office, Mark approached with an unmistakable authority in his bearing. It took no time at all to notice something very different about him.

"Are you being a little presumptuous there?" Clint asked, pointing to the sheriff's badge Mark wore pinned to his shirt. "I didn't hear anything about an election this morning."

"I'm the acting sheriff for the time being," Mark answered. "There isn't anyone here who'll question it."

Clint glanced at the faces of the other lawmen who were gathering between the two buildings. Not all of the deputies were present, but there wasn't a dissatisfied expression on any of the faces of those who were there.

TWENTY-SIX

In truth, Clint would have been more surprised if someone else had taken Charlie's position, but it was good to see that everyone was on the same page. Satisfied with the way things were headed, he said, "All right then, Sheriff. What's our next move?"

"First thing, we make sure our bounty hunters here were telling the truth." With that, Mark raised his left hand, which was holding a rolled-up piece of paper, and stepped toward the jailhouse door.

The younger deputy in charge of the prisoner pushed the jailhouse door all the way open and stepped aside, allowing Mark to pass. Clint followed the new sheriff inside with Willa not far behind. Eldon came in next, escorted by two of the older deputies, who appeared to be in their mid- to-late thirties.

The jail looked as if it had once been a residence. There were stains and scuffs on the floor where furniture had been and food had been spilled. In fact, the place still had the faint odor of baking bread, which had probably seeped into the wood after a kitchen had been there for many years.

Although it might have been a home at one time, it hadn't been a very big one. The cells were only about four feet by six feet. There was enough space for only four of them—two on each side of a central aisle that was barely wide enough for Clint to walk through without having to turn sideways.

Three of the four cells were occupied. The men in them were forced either to lean against the wall or to sit on a little stool that was the only comfort. Clint could smell the alcohol drifting from the first cell and could almost see the fumes coming from the mouth of a man lying unconscious inside.

One of the other men looked drunk as well. In fact, Clint recognized him from the night before at The Rusty Nail. He wasn't unconscious, but he sat on his stool with his hands pressed against his eyes as though he truly wished he was.

The last occupied cell was the second one on the right side. In it was another familiar face, pressed against the bars. The little procession stopped in the aisle. There were six people packed into that narrow space running from the front door to the back of the building, and the space was already beginning to feel like a coffin with bars. Mark stood in front of the prisoner's cell and stared down at him.

The bandit had both hands sticking out through the bars of his cell, held in place by the cuffs that were still locked around his wrists. He was lying on his stomach, and when he moved to look up at the new arrivals, he revealed a face red and bruised from having slept in that position.

" 'Morning, asshole," Mark said with a grin. "Sleep well?" He reached through the bars and took a fistful of hair, jerking the prisoner's head back so that he got a full-on view of his face. With his other hand, he snapped the rolled up paper open to reveal a Wanted poster with a drawn likeness of James Carroll on it.

"It's not a spitting image," Mark said. "But these things never are. And it's old, besides."

Willa and Eldon leaned in a little closer. "It's close enough," she said.

Mark nodded in agreement. "Yeah. It sure is."

Clint looked from the poster's drawing to the man in the cell. The differences between the two were little at best, and could be easily written off as James changing with age or the artist doing his best with witnesses' descriptions. Either way, the man in that cage was most definitely James Carroll.

"What about the rest of them?" Clint asked.

Eldon had moved in directly behind Clint. "The only other one that had a price on his head was Stohls, and he was killed at the bank. By the way," he said, looking at Mark, "when am I gonna get that body so I can take it to get my reward?"

"As soon as we identify it," Mark replied. "I've got a poster with his ugly face on it, too. And another thing . . . you were a help to us at the bank, but so was that lady over there." He pointed at Willa. "If she doesn't get a cut of that money, you'll have to answer to me."

When Eldon looked in Willa's direction, his eyes flashed with a subtle hint of threat. Clint recognized the expression of greed well enough. After all, it wasn't anything that was uncommon, especially among those who made their living cashing in people's souls.

"Sure," Eldon said. "I'll even let her come with me to check on the body. Fair enough?"

Clint looked over to Willa and saw her locking eyes with Eldon. She didn't seem the least bit put off by his warning gaze. In fact, she shot one straight back at him and nodded. "That's fine with me," she said.

Mark looked like he was on the verge of getting frustrated, but he kept his emotions in check. "Good. Now that that's settled, let's get the other identification out of the way. I've seen enough of the undertaker to last me for quite a while."

Instead of simply letting go of James's hair, he threw the bandit's head down so that it smacked against the bars. After everything that had happened, Clint had a hard time finding it in his heart to feel sorry for the prisoner. After all, the outlaw should have felt damn lucky to still be alive. Clint had seen the results of one or two revenge killings, and they were never pretty.

The group filed out of the jailhouse and marched over to the undertaker's parlor. Compared to the cramped confines of the jail, the stifling heat and oppressive humidity felt like a relief. About half a minute later, though, Clint was wiping his brow and readjusting his hat to keep the sun's rays from blazing into his eyes. The relief he'd felt before had melted away like a chip of ice that had been dropped on the ground.

TWENTY-SEVEN

Mark led the procession without a word. He pointed his finger every so often, sending the deputies to various posts around town. Watching the lawman work, Clint had to admire him. He also had to wonder how the hell Charlie had managed to take the job of sheriff out from under him. That had probably been something under Mark's skin as well, and reflected just how good Charlie was at getting on people's good side.

That was a great quality for a politician to have.

It was excellent for a saloon owner and bartender.

It didn't do a sheriff a whole lot of good, though. That much was obvious.

On the way to the undertaker's, Mark rolled up the poster with James's face on it and stuffed it into a pocket of his vest. He traded it for another piece of paper that was folded into a square and appeared to be in much better shape. He unfolded the paper and held it in front of him as they approached a long, narrow building on the edge of town near a good-sized cemetery.

On the poster was a drawing of a man with coal black hair, a shadowy beard and mustache, and mean eyes. The name and laundry list of crimes filled up the bottom half, tagged with a figure in dark numbers.

"Sixty thousand," Mark said, shaking his head. "Thirty if dead. Kind of makes me feel like I'm in the wrong business."

Willa looked at the poster and nodded. She then glanced toward Eldon, who was wearing a nasty smile and looked as though he was about to start drooling on the poster while it was still in Mark's hands. She kept her eyes on him.

The front room of the undertaker's was done up as if the owner was expecting to host a tea party. The chairs were padded with clean velvet and the sunlight beaming through the windows was diffused by curtains made of lace and a soft burgundy fabric. As the group walked inside, their footsteps were muted by a plush area rug that covered most of the floor.

They hadn't been inside the place for a full minute before a tall, plump man with ash blond hair strolled out of a back room. He wore a stained apron over dark pants and a shirt that had probably started off white, but was now a splattered pink. Spots of blood were scattered all over the shirt, and many more were on the apron.

The material was damp with a mixture of perspiration and water that combined to blend the blood into the material like a gruesome kind of dye. The man wrung his hands around a towel, which was stained red, while looking at the new arrivals.

"What can I do for you, Sheriff?" the undertaker asked.

"First off, you can pat yourself on the back, Cal," Mark said. "I think you're the first one in town to call me by my proper title without having to be reminded."

Shrugging, the blood-spattered man finished wiping his hands and tossed the towel onto his shoulder. "I'm reminded of what happened every time I go into my workshop. Sorry about your loss."

Although Cal had probably said those words hundreds of times throughout his career, he managed to keep them close to his heart. When he said them, he looked as though he truly felt them.

"Thanks for that," Mark said. "We need to see the bodies of the men who tried to rob the bank. If it's all right, we can just go back there and look at all of them, since you probably haven't had a chance to—"

"Oh, they're all sorted out," Cal said. "At least . . . as good as I could manage. I separated the familiar faces from the ones I didn't recognize. No need for you to have to go back there and . . . relive the tragedy of what happened."

"Thanks, Cal." Mark seemed to mean those words. As he passed the undertaker, he patted his shoulder, not seeming to mind the blood on his clothes.

Everyone nodded to the undertaker as they walked by. Even Willa and Eldon did so, although they didn't seem to know why. Perhaps it was the friendly way that Cal smiled at them, his face reflecting sincere regret and understanding. Or perhaps it was the fact that he could look so sane and mild-tempered with his clothes covered in gore. Whatever it was, Clint gave a nod to the undertaker as well before heading toward the work space in back.

TWENTY-EIGHT

"You're Clint Adams, aren't you?"

Clint stopped just as he was stepping through the doorway. The smell of blood and rotting flesh was fresh in his nostrils, a wave of stench that slapped against his face. Gladly, he turned away from the smell and looked into the warm face of the undertaker.

"Yes, I am."

"I knew it. I recognized your face."

No matter how friendly the undertaker looked, those words made Clint feel as if he'd been stabbed in the gut with an icicle. Almost immediately, the undertaker shook his head and held out both hands.

"Oh, no, no," he said in a rush. "I didn't mean anything like that. Sometimes I forget that a man in my line of work needs to watch everything he says."

Clint laughed in spite of himself and shook the hand that was being offered to him. "No problem . . . Cal."

Beaming when Clint got his name right, the undertaker slapped his other hand on top of Clint's and shook it again. "That's right. Cal Ackerhauser. What I meant before was that Charlie talked about you an awful lot. He even introduced us once."

"Ackerhauser? That's quite a mouthful. I think I would have remembered that one."

"It was a while back in The Rusty Nail. I'd actually be more surprised if you *did* remember. He spoke highly of you. Charlie, that is."

"I didn't have too many bad things to say about him, either."

"It's a shame what happened."

"Yes, it is."

"I'd like you to rest easy about that, though. He's in my hands now, and I don't mind telling you that I'm fairly good at what I do. He'll be well taken care of. Only the best for Charlie."

"Make sure he gets the best," Clint said. "Money's no object. Whatever the cost . . . I'll cover it when I get back into town."

"No problem. Not at all. It's a pleasure meeting you, sir. A real pleasure indeed. Lord help me . . . but after tending to a good man like Charlie, I don't mind shaking the hands that put those piece-of-shit killers on my table."

Something about the undertaker's tone struck Clint as odd. Perhaps it wouldn't have seemed so strange if it had been said in an angry rasp or even if it had been screamed. But Cal spoke as though he was talking about a good meal or a horse race that had turned out in his favor.

"Thanks for the kind words," Clint said. On his way into the workshop beyond the front parlor, he nodded once again to the portly man with the bloody clothes.

Cal grinned and nodded right back.

When Clint stepped into the workshop, it took him a moment to adjust to the awful stench. It seemed especially harsh in contrast to the flowery scent of the outer parlor. But the decomposing bodies, combined with the sweltering heat that rolled in through the open windows, made the odor overpowering. Following the lead of nearly everyone else in the room, Clint took a handkerchief from his pocket and pressed it against his nose and mouth.

The deputies and bounty hunters were gathered around a rectangular table large enough to hold five men lined up shoulder to shoulder. Another man was stretched out on the floor, baking in the sun. There was a second table just as big as the first, except all of the bodies on that one were covered by a dark tarp and seemed to be lined up with much more precision and care. It was plain that the covered bodies were those of the lawmen. Judging by the way the outlaws were displayed, it was plain what Cal thought about them.

"Let's make this quick," one of the deputies was saying. "I don't want to be in here any longer than I have to."

Mark glared at him over the handkerchief he was using to cover his face. "What the hell do you think I'm doing here? Smelling daisies? Instead of flapping your gums, why don't you help me find that son of a bitch so we can all get out of here?"

Although the lawmen seemed reluctant to get anywhere near the bodies, Willa and Eldon weren't quite so skittish. They had already gotten halfway down the line, and were studying each dead, swollen face with the eyes of experts.

TWENTY-NINE

Clint went over to stand next to Willa, who was at the middle of the table. With the picture he'd seen on the Wanted poster still fresh in his mind, Clint looked over the bodies one by one.

Death had a way of twisting features. Their mouths were open at an odd angle, or their eyes were clouded and swollen like dirty grapes, or their skin was turning a strange color. Cal had done a good job of cleaning them up, but there wasn't much he could do to cover the effects of death.

Some of the bandits had been stripped from the waist up so the undertaker could plug up and clean some of the bigger wounds. Because of that, Clint could see the dark, nearly black tint that the backs of the bodies, which rested on the table, had taken on. He wasn't an expert in such things, but he'd heard that blood settled once the heart stopped. Their chests and faces were pasty white, and the backs were redder than a ripe apple and darker than a shroud.

Thanks to the heat filling the room, the corpses had started to stink. The smell was so bad at times that Clint felt his stomach churning even as he breathed through his clean handkerchief. As much as he wanted to be done with his business here, he forced himself to take his time as he looked at one body, then another, until he finally reached the end of the table.

Eldon and Willa were staring at the body lying there. It took Mark another minute to work his way down there. The other deputies who had come with them had already given up and headed out to the parlor.

"This is him," Eldon said, his voice muffled by the bandanna that covered his face.

The body Eldon was referring to was dressed in plain, dark clothes; his shirt was unbuttoned, but mostly covered his chest. The body looked like a bunch of stuffed clothes spread out on the table. Its skin was pale, and its hands were resting at its sides. Clint thought that body looked closer than any of the others to being asleep . . . until he looked at its head.

The deceased had had a beard. That much was certain. Mark lifted his hand and snapped the poster open so that the picture of Stohls's face was positioned next to the dead man. The new sheriff shook his head and spat out an ironic laugh.

"Of course it is," Mark said. "How could anyone think otherwise?"

Clint looked down at the poster and then at the face Mark compared it to. He didn't think the joke was very funny, though it *was* amusing in a morbid kind of way.

The only real similarity between the corpse and the poster was the beard. It might have helped if the corpse's face hadn't nearly been blown clean off the front of its skull. Above the jaw, there wasn't much besides mashed, pulpy flesh and a blackened crater that marked the spot where Eldon's bullet had entered.

Some of the facial structure remained intact around the

eyes, and along the scalp there was some hair that thickened farther back on top of the head. For the most part, however, Clint figured the undertaker would be better off just painting the glass on the front of that one's casket black.

"What do you think, Clint?" Mark asked as he held the poster a little closer to the corpse. "I'd say it was a spitting image, but I should probably get a second opinion."

"I was the man who shot him," Eldon said. "And I say it was Stohls. Now give me a hand with this here body, and we can get on our way to North Carolina."

The eyes staring over Mark's handkerchief were narrow and filled with a seething energy. After setting the poster down on the corpse's chest, he reached out with that hand and took hold of the older man's shirt. "Take a real good look, you goddamn mercenary," he said, pulling Eldon's face closer to where the corpse's had once been. "Get an eyeful of your handiwork, and be real sure about what you're saying."

Eldon started to resist, but stopped squirming when he saw Clint and Willa both start to move in. He'd already dropped the bandanna, and was now less than an inch away from the remains of a face that looked more like a week-old steak that had been worked over by a couple of starving dogs.

"I see it, I see it," Eldon said, doing his best to keep from inhaling the rank air.

"Can you tell me that that's Kevin Stohls?"

Eldon looked at the bloody face one more time. Fighting to put any distance at all between himself and the corpse, he strained his neck and pulled back against Mark's grip. The sheriff allowed him to back off a bit, but only after the stench had had a good chance to seep into the very bottom of Eldon's lungs.

The bounty hunter stared down at that dead man's face

so hard that Clint couldn't help but take another look for himself. Now that he was more accustomed to the grotesque sight, Clint could start to make out a detail or two hidden beneath the gore. The cheeks had been pretty much blown away, but the facial structure was still there. And though the eyes were nearly covered beneath the mess, they could be seen, too, after a moment or two of effort.

Finally, Eldon smacked the sheriff's hand away and pulled himself back from the table. He looked more humiliated than disgusted by what had gone on, but glared at Mark with a face full of defiance. In a low, steady voice, he said, "I . . . I'm not sure."

THIRTY

"I heard Stohls was close by," Eldon explained. "His gang never does a job without him . . . and James was right there by his side."

"But can you be *sure*?" Mark asked.

"No."

Taking back the poster and folding it up, Mark nodded. "Finally a little bit of straight talk from you."

"I've always been straight with you and . . . the former sheriff."

"Sure, as long as it got you closer to bringing in Stohls so you could make a buck off of him. Your kind makes me—"

"Enough!"

Clint's voice echoed through the workshop with enough force that even the bodies seemed to respond. Eldon and Mark looked annoyed at getting pulled out of their argument when it had just gotten under way. Willa, on the other hand, looked at Clint with a peculiar little grin.

"Sheriff . . . take a look at that body," Clint said.

Mark pulled in a deep breath and leveled his eyes at Clint. "I don't appreciate—"

"And I don't appreciate standing here listening to you two argue. We're here to do a job, so let's get to it. There'll be plenty of time to argue later."

Reluctantly, Mark nodded, lifted his hand, and waved for Cal to come into the room. The undertaker had been waiting patiently at the doorway the entire time, and made his presence known only when he was summoned.

"Could you clean him up a little?" Mark asked.

Cal nodded. "That's just what I was about to do when you all got—"

"Please," Mark said, interrupting the undertaker with a sharp, upraised hand. "Just do it."

With a hand that was quick and professional, Cal swiped a cloth over the corpse's face and dabbed at the little pools of blood that had gathered in the dead man's pores. It was amazing how much blood could be on the body's features without soaking into the flesh. But rather than focus on that, Clint watched as the corpse's face was revealed and some distinguishing features could finally be seen.

Of course, even Cal couldn't do much about the massive damage done to the structure of the skull. But he was an excellent craftsman and eventually cleaned up the shattered head.

Clint was half-expecting the undertaker to make a flourish over the corpse like a magician after performing his newest illusion, but Cal simply bowed his head and faded into the background once again.

Stepping into his former place, Clint looked down at the body. It still wasn't an easy sight to bear, but it was somewhat less disturbing this time around. After Mark held the poster up next to the face, he, Clint, and the bounty hunters made their comparisons.

"I'll be damned," Mark finally said. "Are the rest of you seeing what I'm seeing?"

Willa nodded and stepped back, satisfied enough to leave the room.

Eldon nodded too, shooting a scalding glance toward the sheriff before heading for the door.

That left Clint and Mark alone with the dead. Clint was still looking down at the dead man's face when Mark spoke the very words that were going through his own mind.

"That's Stohls, all right. Or at least . . . close enough for our purposes."

With that decided, the rest of the original group who were still in the workshop were more than happy to file out. Once again, Clint was struck by the contrast between the two rooms. This time, however, the parlor didn't seem friendly and inviting. It seemed overwhelmingly floral and lavish.

Instead of blood and bodies, there were flower arrangements and velvet pillows. Two distinct ends of the spectrum, and Clint was sick of them both. He wasn't the only one thinking along those lines—nobody said a word as they walked through the parlor and headed for the front door.

Before they left, they all looked toward the portly man standing like he was built into the wall, and nodded politely to him before stepping out into the summer heat.

THIRTY-ONE

The air outside was thick with humidity, but it was a definite improvement over what they'd been forced to deal with inside the undertaker's. They all took a moment to breathe deeply and clear the smell of death from their lungs. Once he'd gotten a few welcome breaths of hot, fresh air, Clint turned to the sheriff and asked, "So what's next?"

"Next, we take James down to North Carolina on the first convenient train."

"What about the body in there?" Eldon asked. "It's worth a lot of money to me."

Mark turned to look at the bounty hunter with more weariness than anger in his eyes. "If you want it so badly, then you can go get it. You can also pay to haul it across the country, if that's what you want to do. I'm through with it."

"Fine. Just tell me when we're leaving."

"Oh, you'll be the first person I notify."

Eldon took those words for what they were worth, and stormed back in to see the undertaker. Once he was gone, the sheriff looked at Clint and said, "You've done a lot already. I wouldn't presume to impose on you further."

"I'm in this up to my hips already," Clint said with a shrug. "If you've got something else in mind, I won't object to wading in a little farther."

Mark dismissed his deputy and then took Clint aside where they could talk without being overheard. "I don't have to tell someone like you that we got hit pretty damn hard the other night."

"No, you don't. I was there."

"I'm talking about my deputies and the state of the law in town in general. There's still some good men working for me, and some of the replacements look like they have promise, but only one of the deputies with any real experience survived that shoot-out.

"My duty is to see this through to the end. Now, I know it's the right thing to do, but it would have saved me a hell of a lot of trouble if we had just executed that murdering bastard when we had the chance."

Clint nodded. "Shortcuts don't always go where you want them to, Sheriff. I'm sure I don't have to tell someone like you that kind of thing."

"No, you don't. And I'm not saying I disagree with what happened. The thing is, I need to transport this prisoner and leave the only experienced deputy in charge for a bit. I think he can handle it, but as for the rest of those boys . . . they mean well, but I don't know if they're up to being thrown into the deep end just yet."

"I don't think you have to worry about that bank too much. Anyone else thinking of robbing it will wait until there aren't so many folks talking about what happened there. Plus, folks tend to get awfully protective once they lose so many good men like that."

"That's truer than you know. This morning, I've already had a dozen or so shop owners and businessmen come to me saying they want to get together and be ready to gun down any more robbers in the streets. Hell, I think Abe Landon wants to pull together a militia after he heard what happened to Charlie."

Clint had to smile at that. Even though he'd met the liveryman only once, he didn't have any trouble picturing the short, stocky man backing up a statement like that. "I'm glad to hear that."

"Yeah, well, even though things are pretty well settled here, I'm not too comfortable taking away any able-bodied deputies to accompany me on a train ride with that prisoner."

"Say no more, Sheriff. I was planning on going with you."

Mark let out a breath as though a lead weight had just been taken off his shoulders. "I truly do appreciate it, Mister Adams."

"I think Willa and Eldon should go with us as well."

The relief Mark had just expressed melted from his face the moment he heard that. "I'm not too comfortable with that idea. In fact, I was going to do my best to make sure that bounty hunter misses the train."

"You could do that," Clint said with a shrug. "But both those bounty hunters have a vested interest in making sure the prisoner makes it to where he's headed. And if there are any members of that gang left who want to try to bust him out, or if he gets any ideas of his own to pull something along the way, the first ones to stop him besides us would be Willa and Eldon."

Clint could tell that Mark was warming to the idea, but still needed a bit of encouragement before signing on. "They did a good job last night," he said. "This would be a great way to keep tabs on them . . . and if they come along, they'll be out of Coverdale."

Grudgingly, Mark nodded. "Fine. I think we can handle

this on our own, but since you want them to come along, I'll do it. But just to watch over them. Plus, I like the idea of running them out on a rail . . . even if I have to go with them to do it."

THIRTY-TWO

The train leaving Coverdale for Raleigh, North Carolina, was scheduled to depart at one the following afternoon. Clint spent the time until then not doing a whole lot. He stayed around The Rusty Nail, played some poker, and got some rest. Since every other time he'd tried to relax had blown up in his face, he figured on grabbing some of that time whenever he could. That plan worked a whole lot better.

Since he wasn't tying so hard not to be noticed, he had an easier time blending into the background and staying out of trouble. Clint wasn't the type of man to search out trouble and make a spectacle of himself, but those types of things had a nasty habit of finding him.

However, the worst thing he could think of had already happened, and his friend Charlie Grayson was stretched out on Cal's table. With that already behind him, the world seemed content with leaving Clint alone for the time being.

Late that night Clint excused himself from a low stakes game at one of the tables at The Rusty Nail. He'd enjoyed the company of the others at the game, but for the life of him, he couldn't remember a single name.

The cards hadn't favored him too much that night, but he'd lost less than ten dollars once all accounts were settled. All in all, Clint didn't mind. He said his good-byes, paid for the next round of drinks, and walked out of the saloon.

Clint lifted his chin to the balmy night breeze. He was amazed how it could stay so damn hot when the sun hadn't been in the sky for so long. The summer felt like a ghostly entity with a life all its own, haunting the town and pressing down upon everyone in it.

The hotel where he was staying was less than a block away, and once Clint got to his room, he didn't bother lighting any of the lanterns before dropping onto the bed. His eyelids felt heavy, but sleep was a long way off. He closed his eyes anyway, letting his mind drift for a bit.

He still wasn't anywhere close to falling asleep when someone knocked on his door.

"Yeah?" Clint said without getting up.

The voice on the other side of the door was muffled but unmistakable. "It's me, Clint. Willa."

"What's the full name?"

Clint smiled at the pause that followed.

"Wilhelmina Singer. Now let me in, goddammit."

The room was so small that all Clint had to do was roll over on the bed so he could reach over to unlock the door. Willa came in and shut the door behind her.

"What was that?" she asked. "Some kind of test?"

"No," Clint said, still wearing the grin. "I just like hearing you say your name. It feels like a year since I heard you say it that first time."

"Yeah. A whole lot's been going on since then, hasn't it?"

"So what brings you here?"

"I wanted to apologize . . . for what happened."

"You already did that," Clint said. "And I accepted it."

"That's just the thing. I didn't think you really did, and I feel horrible about what happened." She sat down on the bed next to him. "I feel like I should have done something."

"There was nothing else you *could* do."

"If I had handled this a different way," Willa said, ignoring Clint's last statement, "things might have turned out differently."

"Did you know Charlie before all of this?"

She shook her head. "No. I didn't know him, but he seemed like a good man. I could tell. You may not approve of what I do for a living, but it forces me to be a good judge of character, and I try to keep my jobs as neat as possible. I look into things before I do anything. That way, accidents are less likely to happen." Shaking her head, she added, "Stohls worked that way, too. That's why I thought we had some time before he did anything. That's why I wasn't ready. I thought there was more time, Clint. You've got to believe me."

"I do believe you, Willa." Clint reached out and placed his fingers beneath her chin, moving her head so that she was facing him. "I'm a fair judge of character myself. And *that's* why I would never blame you for what happened."

Suddenly, all of the tension that had been building up inside of her left with a deep exhalation. Her body seemed to deflate a little bit as she lowered herself closer to Clint, who was still lying on the bed. Willa positioned herself so that she was directly above him, propping herself up with a hand on either side of Clint's face.

Her long blonde hair spilled over her shoulders and hung down around her face, enclosing them within a dark golden curtain. Her face was only a few inches from his, and she slowly lowered herself, closing that distance until she was close enough for him to feel her breath on his lips.

"I needed to be close to you tonight," she whispered. "Actually, I wanted to be close to you. I still want that, Clint. I still want you."

"I already forgave you."

"That's not what this is about."

"Then tell me what is."

Willa straightened up so that she was straddling Clint's hips. Slowly, she undid the buttons on her shirt and pulled it open, allowing it to fall off her shoulders. Underneath that, she wore a man's cotton undershirt.

Running her hands down the front of her body, Willa squirmed ever so slightly as her fingers brushed her stiffening nipples. "This is just about me . . . wanting . . . you. Just tell me you don't want me, and I'll leave."

Clint didn't say anything. He let his hands do his talking for him.

THIRTY-THREE

"That two-timing son of a bitch!"

Despite all the noise inside The Rusty Nail, those words could be heard distinctly. The saloon's crowd wasn't new to such language, but the way it was spoken certainly attracted attention. The man who'd thrown the curse into the air spoke with so much feeling that his voice took on a knife's edge that sliced through nearby eardrums.

It came from a man sitting at a table only a few steps from the bar. He sat next to another man, who glared at him with every bit of the intensity that was in his companion's voice.

"Keep it down," the second man said in a low, restrained tone. "Or would you like it if we got spotted here?"

The first man had dark, scruffy hair that nearly reached his shoulders. His skin was coarse and pale—it was obvious that he didn't make much of his living in the sunlight. His features were hard, chiseled into a face made of unyielding stone. His left eye was covered with a frayed black patch, and the right was narrowed to an intense slit.

Dressed in the colors of the night, he wore dark jeans that seemed to soak up the dim light of the room, and his shirt was black as pitch. He wore a black jacket over all of that. In comparison, the silver watch chain dangling from his pocket seemed to be the brightest thing in the room.

"If I was you, I'd watch my own tongue," the one-eyed man said. He didn't have to finish his thought. The implied threat was clear enough in the way every one of his muscles tensed in preparation for the strike.

The other man at the table was dressed in lighter colors. Wearing mostly browns and tans, he blended in with the saloon's customers. His sandy brown hair was just a little shorter than his companion's, and blended seamlessly into a thick beard that spread across his face. There wasn't anything rough about his appearance, but he projected a certain attitude all the same.

His voice had every bit of the edge of the first man's when he said, "We've gone this far without being noticed, and if I have to shoot you to keep it that way . . . make no mistake about it . . . I will."

The tension spiked between them as a silent contest of wills took place. Neither went for his gun right away, and before any other kind of move could be made, one of the serving girls walked up to their table.

"Everything all right over here?" she asked.

The second man let a second tick by, and by the time he turned to look at her, the contest had already been won. "Yes. Everything's fine."

"You boys need anything else to drink?"

"No. We're fine, thanks."

"All right, then." With that, she turned on her heels and bounced off to another table. She swished her hips in a way that normally helped increase her tips, but neither of the men seemed to notice.

Once he knew the girl was no longer paying attention to them, the second man leaned back in his chair and looked away from his companion. "What's gotten into you, Bryce? Are you tired of being a free man? Or, more importantly . . . are you tired of being a *living* free man?"

Bryce Corday leaned forward, both elbows on the table. "You want to know what I'm tired of? I'm tired of sitting around on our asses while that traitorous dog is still walkin' this earth."

His companion's name was Rob Emmerson. He and Bryce had been working together for more years than he could easily remember. They didn't always see eye to eye, but they could deal with each other better than with anyone else. The fact of the matter was that if anyone else had talked to Rob in the tone that Bryce was using, he would be either hurting or dead.

"In case you haven't noticed," Rob said, "that traitorous dog isn't walking anywhere. He's cooling off in a cell, which is right where he should be."

"He should be in a pine box."

"We'll get to that," Rob said. "All in due time."

Bryce balled up his fist and came dangerously close to slamming it down on the edge of the table. With the anger that was boiling up inside of him, if he'd have done that, the entire table would have cracked into two pieces. As it was, he managed to quell his beast before it got too good a hold on him. "Tommy and them others didn't know no better. They was just kids, and that bastard Stohls sent them in to be slaughtered."

"I know. I heard about it same as you."

"Then why haven't we done anything about it? Are you gonna tell me that, or are you just gonna sit there and tell me not to do a damn thing, like you have since we got here?"

"In case you haven't noticed, this whole town's been

crawling with law since we got here. Things are starting to cool down a bit, but there's still deputies posted at just about every corner. If we make a move now, we'll get blasted out of our boots in half the time it took for Tommy to get his."

That last part got Bryce's hackles up, but he didn't do much more than shift in his seat. He appeared to be getting a handle on his rage, and nearly had it stuffed into the dark confines of his soul. "We don't have much time," he said. "The man I talked to said James is gonna be shipped down to Raleigh tomorrow, to face the judge down there."

Rob bristled at the comment, and his mouth twisted into a half-snarl. Like a viper spewing its venom, he spat on the floor. "James won't make it all the way to Raleigh. Any idiot knows that much."

"You think one of them deputies or bounty hunters will kill him?"

"If that was the case, I'd say just leave them to it. Someone's busting him off that train."

"Who would do that? Stohls is dead, isn't he?"

"It doesn't matter if he is or not. They would have arranged for that either way."

"What do you mean?"

"Every account I heard about what happened last night makes it look like one of the sloppiest jobs on record. Stohls doesn't pull sloppy jobs, which means he threw it on purpose. Just because he happened to get caught in it himself doesn't mean James would be left behind. They had something else planned."

"And Tommy got caught in the middle of it."

Rob nodded. "That's right. Stohls and James used him as cannon fodder, knowing damn well what was coming."

"Which brings me to what I was saying before. He's a two-timing son of a—"

This time, Rob stopped Bryce's tirade before it got started with a simple turn of his hand. As soon as he held up one palm, Bryce went quiet before venting everything that was building up inside of him.

"Save it," Rob said. "There'll be plenty of time to use that anger once we catch up to the men responsible for what happened. Your sources said James was being shipped out on tomorrow's train to Raleigh?"

"That's right."

"Then that's where we'll catch up with them."

Bryce smiled. It was an expression that didn't look altogether comfortable on his face. "And how do you suppose we'll do that? Join the posse?"

"No. We'll buy tickets."

THIRTY-FOUR

Unlike the first time Clint had been so close to Willa, he had the luxury of time as well as place. The memory of their last encounter would hold a special place in his dreams, but this time was already shaping up to be just as memorable for its own reasons.

Willa seemed to think so, too; all of her movements were slow and deliberate. She let her hands inch over his body as if the only things she was aware of came through her fingertips. Her breasts swayed freely beneath her undershirt, and she savored the sensation of her nipples brushing against the fabric. When Clint reached up to rub the palms of his hands along them, she drew in a quick breath and let it out slowly.

Neither of them talked. At least, not at first. The sound of their breathing was enough for the moment, especially when coupled with the creak of the bed. There was just enough coming through the window for Clint to make out the shape of Willa's figure and a few intimate details. Beyond that, they were both two shadows converging in the night.

They were in no hurry this time. They had nothing else

to think about except pleasing each other. Clint moved his hands beneath Willa's shirt, brushing over the thin fabric of her undershirt. He savored the feel of her feminine curves beneath masculine clothing. Finally, when he couldn't deny himself any longer, he pulled the shirt completely off of her and tugged the undershirt up over her head.

Willa smiled and squirmed on top of him, moving her hands down along the sides of her breasts, massaging them until she felt Clint's touch on her once again. Leaning her head back, she pulled Clint's shirt open and worked her fingers along the muscles of his chest and shoulders.

Clint reached up and took hold of her, rolling them both onto their sides. As his hands explored her body, she reacted to his touch on her stomach . . . then her sides . . . then the edges of her hips . . . and finally the inside of her thighs.

Reflexively, Willa's legs moved open so Clint could bring his hand closer to her moist vagina. She let out a contented moan the moment she felt his fingers grazing her tender lips, moving up along them until he touched her clitoris.

Keeping her eyes closed and her head thrown back, she pulled Clint's jeans open and tugged them down until she could get them all the way off. He undressed her as well, tearing her remaining clothing off with a passionate desperation. Once that was done, Willa positioned herself on her side again and waited for Clint's fingers to find the fine hair between her legs.

Clint knew what she wanted, and didn't hesitate to give it to her. This time, he slipped one finger inside . . . then two . . . and gently eased them all the way in until Willa shuddered with a wave of pleasure. Her hands were busy as well, stroking his cock slowly, mimicking the rhythm of Clint's fingers moving between her legs.

She suddenly moved away from him, lowering her head so she could take him inside her mouth. Willa's full, soft lips closed around his shaft as her tongue swirled around its tip. She looked up at him as she slid farther down, swallowing his hard cock and then slowly moving her lips up along its length.

For the next few seconds, Clint leaned back and enjoyed her attention. He felt chills run down his spine as she tightened her lips around him while bobbing her head up and down. As she worked on him, Clint moved so he could once again reach between her legs and finger her pussy. When he hit the right spot, she arched her back and started moaning with him still in her mouth.

Clint pulled her closer, and she crawled on top of him. The moment she took her lips away from his penis, she wrapped one hand around it, stroking slowly. Willa straddled Clint's chest, grinding her hips against him as he massaged the succulent curves of her buttocks. He slipped his fingers between her thighs, teasing the damp, tender skin there with a few fleeting touches.

Although he couldn't see it, Clint could picture the smile on Willa's face. She bent down and flicked her tongue along the length of his penis, brushing her lips over the tip but refusing to take him inside.

Finally, Clint could take no more. He pulled her closer until she was straddling his face. Her legs spread wide, and she lowered herself until Clint could bury his mouth in her dripping pussy. Willa let out a throaty groan as Clint thrust his tongue inside of her. Just when it seemed she was going to run out of breath, she dropped her head and wrapped her lips around his cock.

As Clint worked his tongue in and out of her, she sucked on him with the same intensity. They could feel themselves racing toward a climax, but didn't want to get there just yet.

Clint stopped tasting her, and Willa got up, turned around, and lowered herself onto his rigid pole. They both moaned with satisfaction as she took him all the way inside her. Willa bent at the knees and rode him while keeping her hands on his chest.

Clint grabbed her by the hips, guiding her pumping motions while savoring the feel of her muscles tensing. When he started thrusting his hips upward and pumping into her even harder, Willa tossed her hair from side to side, completely lost in the sensations that flowed through her body.

Clint could feel her pussy tightening around him, as well as the erotic scraping of her fingernails pressed into his skin. Her entire body shook with her orgasm, and she ground her hips against him the entire time, rubbing herself against his erection until she could hardly move.

Clint wasn't quite through with her yet. He reached up and supported her while rolling her onto her back. Once he got onto his knees, he spread her legs and moved closer. Willa might have been weak for the moment, but she wanted to feel him inside her again. As soon as she felt his cock pressing against her moist pussy, she set her feet on his shoulders and guided him all the way inside.

Clint slid into her easily, thrusting his hips forward, and started pounding in and out. Her breath coming in short gasps, Willa grabbed the mattress with both hands and pushed her head back into the pillow. She was feeling another climax approaching, but all she could do was hold on and pump her hips to Clint's rhythm as he drove into her again and again.

Clint exploded inside of her, letting out a satisfied moan that was drowned out by the cries of passion coming from

Willa. Once those passed, Clint pulled out of her and collapsed onto the bed.

For the next couple of moments, they just lay there and listened to the sound of their own breathing. The room was hot, but it was the heat they'd generated themselves, and thus a whole lot easier to bear. Finally, Willa curled up next to Clint and draped one arm over his chest.

Their naked bodies came together and they drifted off to a contented sleep. They woke up a few hours later and immediately made love again. They stayed on their sides, and Willa hooked her leg up and over Clint's hips so he could enter her.

They slid against each other, the sweat from their skin mingling as he thrust between her legs. This time, when they were done, neither of them had the energy to do anything but hold the other and fall back asleep, figuring they wouldn't get another chance to relax for quite a while.

THIRTY-FIVE

Clint didn't know exactly how well Charlie was liked until he and Willa met the new sheriff and Eldon at the train platform the next day. He and Willa were there a little early, but the train to Raleigh was already there, steaming on the tracks.

Figuring that Mark wouldn't be there until the last minute, Clint hadn't allowed himself to get too anxious. Willa, on the other hand, was another story.

"Shouldn't they be here by now?" she asked, shifting from one foot to the other.

"The sheriff said he wanted to go straight from the jailhouse to the train, and he doesn't want to sit around waiting to leave."

"I know, but shouldn't we be there with them?"

"No. He wanted us here in case anyone sets up an ambush or something like that. You were there when we talked to him over breakfast, weren't you?"

"Yeah, I was there. It's just that I don't like waiting around while things happen without me."

"A lot of things happen without you, Willa."

Still focusing on the road leading to the platform, Willa

smacked Clint's arm with the back of her hand. "You know what I mean."

Clint didn't take offense at the blow. In fact, he barely felt it. While he was better at hiding his anxiousness, Clint was still feeling it mighty strongly. "Well, fidgeting and arguing here isn't going to speed things up any. Why don't you check the area once again to see if there's any sign of trouble?"

"We both checked it twice already."

"Then take a run around the station," Clint said. "Tire yourself out a little before you jump out of your skin. Or would you rather I tire you out?"

Willa turned and touched his arm. She looked up into his eyes and smiled alluringly. "Better watch your tongue, mister. If you make promises you don't intend on keeping, I just might have to hurt you."

"Save that for later. We've got a job to do."

Willa nodded and turned to look once again at the people milling about on the platform. She knew from experience that anything could happen at any time. She and Clint both knew that James Carroll was a wanted man. Besides the vigilantes gunning for his hide, there was always the possibility that other members of his gang would attempt to free him.

Anything at any time.

It was something Clint kept in the back of his mind as well. During some of his "relaxing" time, he'd done some research on Stohls's gang. Word of mouth put Stohls at damn near the top of the criminal trade. He'd pulled off robberies of all sorts, and had killed close to half the men he'd ever met. Newspaper clippings backed up enough of those stories for Clint to be concerned. At the very least, he was convinced it was a good idea to make sure the transfer to North Carolina proceeded carefully.

James Carroll was a dangerous man in his own right.

If he went on this train with only one or two men to look after him, there was a good chance he could cause plenty of damage on his own. Clint felt bad enough about what happened to Charlie. He wasn't about to sit back and let his replacement get hurt as well.

Besides . . . Clint was starting to like the way Mark ran things.

"Hey! Look sharp over there!"

The voice came from the side of the small building where tickets were purchased and reservations were made. Because she was already looking in that direction, Willa responded to it first, her hand dropping immediately to the .45 holstered at her hip.

Clint spotted the figure a split second later, recognizing the portly man who was running around the building, dragging something behind him. "Hold up," he said, placing his hand over Willa's before she managed to clear leather. "No need to shoot this one just yet."

Willa kept the gun where it was, but still stared intently at the man, who was now running straight for them. She moved next to Clint as he started walking toward the oncoming man.

At first, it had looked like the man was dragging something behind him. But as soon as Abe Landon cleared the building with Eclipse's reins in his hand, the roles quickly reversed. The instant the Darley Arabian saw Clint's face, he burst into a trot that nearly rolled right over the liveryman.

Clint patted the stallion on the nose as soon as he was within reach. In turn, Eclipse nuzzled his face and shook his head.

"Looks like he missed you," Abe said.

"He's about due for a run, is all. It feels like I haven't laid eyes on this one for a month." Clint scratched Eclipse's ears for another second or two before taking the reins from Abe's hands. "How much do I owe you?"

"Not a cent, Mister Adams. I heard about all you did, and I'd like to offer my personal thanks."

The liveryman thrust out a meaty paw, which Clint accepted and shook.

"Would you like me to load him onto the train for ya?"

"No," Clint said. "I don't mind doing it myse—" He stopped in midsentence as another group of familiar faces appeared around the station building. "On second thought," Clint said without taking his eyes from the newest arrivals, "I'd appreciate it if you did see Eclipse to the train."

Abe gladly accepted the reins and turned to look at what was catching Clint and Willa's attention. The first one in sight was Eldon Masters. Directly behind him was James Carroll his hands secured behind his back, walking in front of the sheriff.

"That bloodthirsty bastard," Abe spat. "I hope he gets what's comin' to him."

Clint stepped past the liveryman and placed his hand on the modified Colt at his side. "Don't fret about it, Abe. We'll certainly do our best."

THIRTY-SIX

"There he is," Bryce Corday said as he looked away from Clint and shifted his gaze toward the sheriff's small procession. "We should take him down right now."

Rob stopped him with a firm grip on his elbow. They were on a section of the platform that was in the middle of the flow of traffic going to and from the train. Passengers walked by them on all sides while other folks stood around, waiting to meet friends or relatives.

Bryce nearly bolted the moment he got a look at James's face.

"Be patient," Rob hissed. "We want to make them all pay for what they done . . . the whole gang. Not just this one. Between us and the law, he's dead already."

"Then what the fuck are we waiting for?"

"If there are any more of Stohls's men out there, this transfer will flush them out. Besides . . . are you forgetting about all of those other jobs this one and Stohls pulled together?"

"No," Bryce snarled, his eyes following the prisoner across the platform. "How could I forget, with you reminding me all the time?"

"Then why don't you take a look at James over there? Take a good look for a moment."

Bryce did, but he still needed to be restrained from taking off after the prisoner.

"Does he look like a rich man?" Rob asked.

"No."

"Well, he is. So was Stohls. And since they didn't have nice clothes or even a permanent place to live, as far as anyone knows, that means most of the money they stole is still sitting somewhere, waiting to be claimed."

That stopped Bryce from trying to lunge forward. Instead, he turned and fixed his partner with an intent stare.

"Ahhh," Rob said with a nod. "*Now* I see the light coming on in there. Since we're already on this ride and we're already going to pay James a visit, we might as well get something for our trouble."

"And I suppose you think he'll just tell us where the stash is?"

"Not without a little encouragement, but that's where you can take over. Once we get James to ourselves, and if he doesn't feel cooperative, you can make him pay with a pound of flesh for what he did to Tommy. And you can cut that flesh from any part of him you want."

Bryce nodded slowly, every one of his muscles easing back as though he was suddenly drifting into a comfortable sleep. "Now I like the sound of that. Are you sure about that stash of money?"

"It makes sense. And if we don't find any cash, we know for sure we'll get what we want."

"True enough."

The procession accompanying James Carroll was getting dangerously close to the spot where Bryce and Rob were standing. The pair of gunmen turned their faces before they were noticed, and the crowd kept flowing around them.

As far as Rob could tell, they hadn't attracted any undue attention. Also, there were enough last-second passengers moving onto the train that it would have been hard to pick out a familiar face in the crowd.

Once the last of the sheriff's group had gotten on the train, Bryce and Rob stepped on board as well. The conductor took their tickets, tipped his hat, and wished them a good trip. The two gunmen settled into their seats just as the engine let out a loud whistle and lurched into motion.

Whenever anyone looked at the seats next to them, Bryce shot them a look that could have burned a hole through the side of the car. Before long, the passengers were in their places and the train was picking up speed.

"When do we make our move?" Bryce asked.

Rob was staring out the window, watching the last traces of Coverdale slide away. "Don't worry about it yet. We'll play it as it comes."

"We can't wait too long. Not with Clint Adams keeping company with the sheriff."

"Forget about Adams. He doesn't know we're here. First thing we have to do is get a good look at where the sheriff is holding James and how that prick is being guarded. After that . . . we just wait for an opportunity."

"Yeah . . . well, I can't wait that long."

Rob closed his eyes and leaned his head back against the back of his seat. "Don't worry . . . you won't have to."

THIRTY-SEVEN

The loading process went fairly smoothly. Mark brought the prisoner from the jailhouse and onto the train without a hitch. James didn't put up much of a fuss, and had only a few stains on his clothing from where a local farewell committee paid their respects with some rotten fruit and mud. Eldon was continuing to look after the prisoner, as he'd done during the trip to the train platform.

Eclipse was making the trip in relative comfort. The Darley Arabian had half the livestock car to himself since most of the passengers weren't the type to bring their horses along for the ride. The other passengers were mostly businessmen and families headed for Raleigh. They stared at the sheriff and James hard, but the novelty wore off before long.

Clint sat in the last row of seats in the last open passenger car. Right behind him was the door leading to the sleeper car that consisted of three small, private rooms. Each room was just big enough for a bed, a small table and a couple of chairs. The sheriff had booked the entire car, using money that he intended on getting back once the bounty hunters received their reward. He called it a "traveling tax," since neither of them had paid for their tickets.

The longer he was around the newly appointed sheriff, the more Clint liked the guy. He always seemed to figure an angle for something. Also, Mark wasn't unfamiliar with planning the particulars of the prisoner transfer. At that moment, he was briefing Willa in the private car, no doubt grilling her several times regarding timetables and procedures. In that respect, Clint was glad his place was in another car.

Once the passengers had settled down, Clint could see that the train wasn't completely full. In his car, just over half the seats were taken. Of course, once word had spread about James Carroll being on the train, most folks found seats in the car farther up, away from where the prisoner was being held.

That suited Clint just fine, since it meant he had fewer people to watch. As soon as he thought that, the door at the front of the car swung open and some passengers squeezed through. The timing made Clint wonder if those people would have showed up if he hadn't thought about not wanting them to.

Some people said the world was a strange place. Clint didn't think so. Most of the time, it pushed when he pulled, or vice versa. Nothing too hard about that. Nothing much to be happy about, either, but there *was* something to be said for simplicity.

Clint watched two men enter the car and noticed something familiar about one of them right away. He couldn't quite put his finger on it, but he might have seen him somewhere before. On the other hand, after seeing so many different faces on and around the train platform, Clint might very well have seen him just before the train pulled away from the station.

Not one to doubt his hunches, Clint noted where that

man and his companion sat down, just in case he spotted one of them somewhere he didn't belong. For the time being, both men seemed content to find a seat toward the front of the car and talk to each other once they were settled.

Clint was just about to check on what was happening in the sleeper car when the connecting door came open and Willa stepped through. The look on her face reminded Clint of someone who'd just come in from a storm and was glad to be alive. She dropped into the seat beside him, letting out a huffing breath.

"Did Mark tell you what you needed to know?" Clint asked.

She slowly turned to look at him and then let out a short, gasping laugh. "He told me so much that I needed to know, I feel like I could run for the job of sheriff myself."

"I had a feeling that might be the case. He seems like a very thorough sort."

"That's one word for it. I wouldn't get too comfortable if I were you. Your turn's probably coming up fairly soon."

"After seeing what he did to you, I'm almost hoping James tries to escape. That would keep Mark busy until we reach North Carolina."

Rubbing her eyes with the palms of her hands, Willa said, "He was in the room when I got some of my speech. Mark made sure not to say anything important, but I'm sure James heard enough to put him to sleep for at least a day or two. I'd be surprised if he still had a will to live, not to mention enough gumption left to escape after going through that."

Clint laughed at what she said just as much as how she said it. Judging by the tone of her voice and the weariness in her body, a person might think that she'd just run a couple of miles to catch up to the train instead of sitting in one of its most expensive cars. It wasn't long before Willa was laughing right along with him, and they both enjoyed the moment while they could.

The seats in the passenger car weren't the best, but they were padded and beat the hell out of a saddle. As the train clattered over the rails, it made a steady tapping noise that had already started to lull Clint into a relaxed state.

"It's been a while since I've traveled on one of these," Clint said, snapping his eyes open and forcing himself to sit up straight. "I nearly forgot how soothing it was."

"Yeah. Real soothing. The cars are cramped and stink of sweat because there're usually more people packed in here than cattle in a stall. The seats are worn through so that you wind up sitting on bare wood and getting splinters in your ass. And don't even open the windows, or you'll probably get a hot cinder in your eye."

"I take it you travel by train pretty often?"

"A little too often."

"Then try riding more," Clint said. "It'll make you appreciate things a little more."

"Is that so? Appreciate things like . . ." Suddenly, Willa's voice trailed off, leaving her sentence dangling like a thread in midair.

Clint looked away from the window. She was staring toward the front of the car. "What is it?" he asked.

When she spoke again, she lowered her voice to something just half a notch over a whisper. "One of those men up there . . . toward the front of the car. He was looking back here."

"So?"

"I didn't like it."

It wasn't much, but when Clint looked over at Willa, he could almost feel the instinctual twisting in her guts which accompanied the feeling that something just wasn't right. He'd had that feeling several times himself, and it was never easy to explain it to someone else. It was something someone either felt or didn't feel . . . there was no explaining it.

And when Clint looked down the length of the car at the two men who'd walked in earlier, he was reminded of that gut feeling because he felt it himself. They were still the same pair he'd seen a few minutes ago, but there was something about them this time that just wasn't right.

"How long have they been here?" Willa asked.

"Not long. They just walked in. I didn't think too much of them at first."

"I don't know . . . something about the way one of them looked back here caught my eye."

Clint stayed quiet until one of the men turned and glanced toward him. Their eyes met for a split second before the man turned around in his seat.

"Stay here," Clint said. "I'll check it out. You watch my back."

"Be careful, Clint. I have a bad feeling about this."

THIRTY-EIGHT

"He's coming over here," Rob said after Bryce had turned around in his seat.

Bryce's hand drifted slowly toward his gun. The motion was subtle and smoother than a snake flowing through the grass, but Rob caught sight of it all the same—because Bryce had wanted him to see what he was doing.

In a motion just as subtle, Rob shook his head once. That was enough to get his message across. Bryce, looking none too happy about it, pulled his fingers away from the handle of his pistol and drew his hand up beneath the arm crossed over his stomach.

The sound of footsteps drew closer, and a hand landed upon the back of Bryce's seat.

"Good day to you, gentlemen," Clint said as he looked down at the two men.

Bryce didn't look up. Instead, he stared straight ahead, leaving the conversation to Rob. After all, each had his specialty, and this wasn't the time for Bryce to exercise his own particular talent. That would come soon enough.

Glancing up at Clint as though he'd just pulled himself away from something terribly interesting, Rob blinked his eyes and put on a tired smile. "Hello. Is there something I can do for you?"

Clint put on an amiable grin of his own. All the while, he studied both men carefully. Not a single move they made or expression that crossed their faces went unnoticed. "Just stretching my legs. You know how that goes."

"Yeah. I was just trying to catch some sleep, myself."

"Well, I don't want to interrupt you. I was just checking to make sure you knew the situation that's going on in the next car."

A flicker passed across Rob's face, almost as though his smile was a mask that disappeared for a split second to reveal what was going on underneath. If someone hadn't been looking for it, the brief glimpse might have been mistaken for a twitch or even a trick of the light. But Clint knew exactly what he was looking for, and that flicker told him a hell of a lot.

"Situation?" Rob said as the twitch flashed over his features. "I saw the sheriff escorting a man back there, but I don't pretend to know what it was about. We're not from around here. Is there a problem of some kind?"

"Not at the moment. But you know how these things go. Once something starts getting spread around, sooner or later people get edgy. We just want to assure you that, no matter what you've heard, everything's fine."

Bryce turned in his seat to get a look at Clint. His eyes were narrow slits, but they were a fountain of information for Clint. Once he turned back around, Bryce let out a breath and straightened his back.

"Well, we haven't heard much," Rob said convincingly. "If you say there's nothing to worry about, we're glad to hear it. Thanks for putting our minds at ease."

Clint tipped his hat. "That's what we're here for. Be sure to spread the word if someone does start talking about the subject."

"Certainly."

"My name is Clint," he said, extending his hand. "If you need me for anything, I'll be right back there."

Rob shook Clint's hand and nodded. "Extend my thanks to the sheriff as well. He seems to be doing a fine job. At least . . . that's what we've been hearing."

"Will do. Enjoy the rest of the ride."

Leaning forward a bit to look down into Bryce's face, Clint tipped his hat as soon as he saw he'd gotten his attention. Without further delay, he walked back up the aisle, nodding to the few passengers who looked up as he passed by.

Clint took a seat opposite Willa, so that he was facing the sleeper car.

"Fifty cents says they get up and walk out of here within a minute," he said under his breath.

Willa's eyes darted from Clint to the men sitting at the opposite end of the car. "Did you say something to them that everyone in this car couldn't hear?"

"No."

"Did you threaten them . . . with your eyes or something?"

Clint's laugh was genuine, and it shook his shoulders gently. "Nope."

She thought for a second, looked at the men, and then back to Clint. "A minute from then or from now?"

"There's about thirty seconds left."

"I'll take that bet."

Almost as soon as she had whispered her acceptance, Willa's face dropped, and she started shaking her head. Clint didn't have to look, but he did anyway, shifting in his seat so he could peek down the aisle.

Sure enough, both of the men he'd spoken to were getting up and walking toward the door that led to the second passenger car. Wearing a self-satisfied smirk on his face,

Clint leaned back in his seat and held his hand out to Willa.

"I believe you owe me some money," he said once the pair of men had shut the door behind them.

Willa slapped two quarters onto his waiting palm. "What was that all about? How did you know that was going to happen?"

"Well, the one I talked to was good at keeping himself in check, but he was definitely anxious about something. He was even more anxious when I hinted that there might be unrest in the sheriff's camp."

"Really? What did he say?"

"It wasn't what he said. Just how he looked when he said it."

In her profession, Willa was very familiar with that line of reasoning. "And what about the other one?" she asked.

"Oh, he was fine, too, until I dropped that hint. When he turned around to face me, I thought he might be ready to jump, but he kept his composure . . . just barely. That one's ready to start something. The only thing holding him back is his friend who does the talking.

"Just to be sure, I told them my name. Neither one of them looked like they were going to draw on me, but they both had been thinking about it. I could see that in their eyes."

So many men had wanted to kill Clint just for who he was that he'd learned to practically smell it in the air. The scent had been subtle, but it had definitely been there, hanging over the head of those two men.

"So what should we do?" Willa asked. "I could tell those two were up to something just by the way they looked back here. We can't let them walk around without keeping an eye on them. And it would be stupid to wait for them to make their move. Believe me, I know."

"You make it your business to know names and faces. Are those two part of Stohls's gang?"

Willa shook her head. "I've never seen them before. But Stohls was known to have a lot of people working for him in towns all over the country."

"We need to find out for sure. Maybe the sheriff or Eldon could have a look."

Just then, the door to the sleeper car opened and a haggard Eldon Masters came out. "Maybe I should have a look at what?"

THIRTY-NINE

Clint and Eldon stood on the small platform between the two passenger cars. As soon as he'd heard what Clint suspected about the two men, Eldon wanted to move right away and see if he might have better luck identifying them. All the while, he was stretching his arms and back, rolling his head around on his shoulders.

"Hold up here for a second," Eldon said as Clint was about to open the second door. "I need a few breaths of fresh air."

Clint let go of the handle and stepped next to Eldon, who was leaning against the iron railing that kept them from tumbling off the train. The clatter of wheels on rails filled the air as it rushed by. The chugging of the engine was a constant thrum, punctuated every once in a while by the shriek of a whistle.

For a second or two, they stood there and watched the scenery race by. When they looked out, the green of leaves and grass moved past at a steady, leisurely pace. When they looked down, however, the browns of dirt and grays of stone and metal were moving so quickly that they were nothing but a blur. The wind even seemed to assault them harder when they focused on the speeding ground as opposed to the trees in the distance.

Eldon pulled in a few deep breaths and let them out.

"The sheriff was grilling you pretty bad, huh?" Clint asked sympathetically.

"You know, the way that man talks to me, you'd swear he figured I belong in chains right beside that killer in there."

"He's a lawman. A lot of them don't take to well to men in your profession."

"Maybe I should make it a little easier on him."

When Eldon said that, Clint's instincts told him that the flicker of menace he saw in the other man's eyes could very well be annoyance with the way Mark had been treating him. Then again . . . Before Clint could think about that flicker, it was gone, thrown off and forgotten.

"All right," Eldon said as he straightened up and turned toward the second door. "We've got a job to do. Let's get back to it."

It wasn't until Clint opened the door leading into the other passenger car that he realized just how empty the first one was. Compared to the one he'd just left, this car was full to brimming with passengers of every size, shape, and age.

There were kids running up and down the aisles, old folks grumbling to each other while playing cards, and everyone in between, either milling about or sleeping in their seats. The train had been rolling for only a couple of hours, but the air already had a stale taste to it after having been through so many different sets of lungs.

Clint stepped into the car and moved on, allowing Eldon to get inside behind him. Already he was yearning for the relative solitude of the other car, and had to step aside several times within the first few paces in order to get out of the way of half a dozen people. Even the heat seemed worse in there, stoked by the bodies that were crushed together inside the huge box on wheels.

"Where did you say those two were?" Eldon asked from behind Clint.

"They went in here, but suddenly I'm feeling like an idiot for not following them directly."

Clint felt a pat on his shoulder, and Eldon squeezed past him. "Don't fret yourself," Eldon said. "I'm used to weeding through haystacks like this one. We'll find them two needles."

Once Eldon took the lead, Clint fell in behind him. He didn't mean for the older man to take over, but now that he had, Clint saw right away that the bounty hunter was happy to be doing something on his own. He walked down the narrow space between the two sets of seats, glancing from one side to the other, and studying each face in turn. Even though Eldon hadn't seen the other two, he knew what he *wasn't* looking for.

Whenever he came across a man who wasn't elderly or in knickers, the bounty hunter glanced back at Clint, who took a look. Through the first half of the car, Clint dismissed the men Eldon pointed out almost immediately. He let the older man keep up his search, however, since he was doing a great job of parting the flow of humanity and clearing the path for him to follow. Also, Clint figured it was better if his wasn't the first face those two men spotted.

Of course, if they were in there, those two would have spotted them as soon as they'd walked through the door.

It was obvious that Eldon figured that much as well, since he kept one hand resting on his gun while the other took hold of each bench as he walked by. When he got to the next-to-last bench, Eldon stopped. "Clint . . . one o'clock."

Clint looked at the seat ahead and to his right. It was

the last one in line, and it was also the emptiest. The only thing that could be seen over the back of the bench was a pair of hats that Clint found very familiar.

"Careful," Clint whispered. His words were instantly swallowed up by the noise inside the car, but Eldon nodded to show that he'd caught them. "Go in nice and slow."

Clint stayed a few steps behind so that Eldon would have a little bit of a head start. So far, the two men seemed to be content sitting in their places and looking straight ahead. But Clint knew better than to take that at face value. He could only hope that Eldon was doing the same.

The bounty hunter moved to the end of the front bench and looked at the men sitting there. "Howdy, friends. Mind if I—"

"I'll be god damned," Bryce said in a raspy snarl.

Rob had already turned to look, and was in the process of reaching for his gun. "It's you!"

FORTY

Clint had had a bad feeling in the pit of his stomach ever since he'd first laid his eyes on those two. Even before Bryce went for his weapon, Clint knew that something was going to happen, and that it wasn't going to be good. Before he could do anything to prevent it, both of the men seated on the bench were about to clear leather, and Eldon was right there with them.

The bounty hunter's hand was already on the .44 at his side, and he drew the pistol with one fluid motion. And by the time Bryce and Rob had their guns drawn, they were on their feet and spinning around to face Clint and Eldon.

"Get down!" Clint shouted. His voice filled the car like suffocating smoke, and most of the passengers dropped to the floor.

Even as he yelled his warning, Clint hadn't taken his eyes off the two men in front of him. Since there were two of them, he had to decide which one needed to be dealt with first . . . and he had less than a second to choose.

Bryce was the first one out of his seat. Throwing himself to one side while wheeling his upper body around, he brought up his gun and squeezed off a shot without pausing to take aim. That was the only thing that saved Eldon's life as the gun roared and delivered its fiery lead into the bench less than an inch from Eldon's side.

Clint was the next one to fire. Aiming more by instinct than anything else, he sent a round into Bryce's upper body that spun him around like a child's toy and slammed him against the front of the car. Even as the Colt's bark was still thundering in his ears, Clint was turning his attention toward the second man.

Although he'd managed to clear leather, Rob wasn't about to take his own shot just yet. He was more concerned with the bullet coming at him from the barrel of Eldon's gun. The bounty hunter's .44 spat smoke with a flicker of fire that resembled a serpent's tongue lashing out in the wake of the hot lead that now whipped through the air.

Rob hadn't stood all the way up, and was already tossing himself back onto the bench. He dived toward the uncomfortable wooden surface as though diving into a pond, holding both arms outstretched over his head and lowering his face reflexively from the blast.

Although Rob had been thinking quickly on his feet, there wasn't a man alive who could have avoided that bullet before it drilled into his flesh. The searing hot metal turned in a tight spiral like the sharp end of a corkscrew. Rob felt it the instant it touched his skin after tearing through the back of his shirt.

The bullet dug a painful, bloody trench across his shoulder blade until it hit bone. From there, the slug changed its course slightly and burrowed deeper into Rob's back as though seeking a warm place to hide. It took less than a second to inflict the wound, but Rob felt the round dragging through him like an animal's claw.

When his chest hit the bench, he let out a muffled scream and fought through the blackness that crept into the edge of his field of vision.

When Bryce slammed against the front of the car, he stayed there for a moment, wincing in pain. Already he could feel his blood flowing out through a wound in his shoulder and sticking to the wall behind him. He knew without looking that the round had gone all the way through him, leaving a messy hole in its wake.

Rather than let the pain get to him, Bryce gritted his teeth and used it to fuel him onward. Eldon's face was still burning in his mind, but it had been the other one who'd shot him. Thinking like a wounded animal, Bryce turned his eyes toward Clint and raised his gun to take aim.

Already moving for cover, Clint saw what Bryce was about to do just as another movement caught his attention: a flicker of contrast between light and dark from between the slats of the bench's backrest.

Rob was peeking out from behind there. And so was the barrel of his gun.

Clint's mind worked so fast, thanks to his reflexes, that he felt as though he was watching things after they'd been slowed down. Even so, he barely had a chance to react before Rob took a free shot at his gut. Clint wasn't about to waste a shot if he wasn't sure what he was aiming at, and the bench's slats were hiding just enough of Rob to make that the case.

So Clint made a decision and went against one of his deeply held beliefs. Turning at the waist with his gun held in one hand, he squeezed the trigger several times in quick succession, blasting holes into the bench without hitting a damn thing.

He'd wasted ammunition when he needed it the most, but he'd also stopped Rob from shooting at him. Using the opening he'd created, Clint stepped back and to one side, rushing out of the aisle and dropping into a low crouch behind a bench.

At that moment, Rob's body slammed against the floor. He appeared unconscious for a brief second, but then he rolled to one side, confirming his wound wasn't as bad as it could've been.

Bryce, on the other hand, was another story. He was straightening up and walking into the open because he had already been bloodied. He moved with a strength that flowed from having nothing to lose. The front of Bryce's shirt was nearly black with blood, yet he somehow managed to keep moving.

Clint saw Bryce coming, and watched as he pulled a second pistol from where it had been stashed in his gun belt. The holdout gun was older and smaller, but it filled his left hand all the same, and was ready to fire when Bryce thumbed back its hammer.

Clint also saw the purposeful way that Bryce walked toward him and Eldon, ignoring the pain from his wounds. But what Clint noticed most was that Bryce's eyes had become dull and lifeless. They were the eyes of a walking dead man who was intent on making sure that he didn't go to his grave alone.

FORTY-ONE

Clint set his mind to putting Bryce down like the wounded dog he was, and was set to do so until he saw Rob roll out from behind the bench and lunge for the next row of seats. Sitting there was an elderly woman who had been covering her head with her hands. The moment she saw Rob coming, she let out a piercing shriek that rattled through the entire car.

"Shut your mouth," Rob snarled as he took hold of her around her neck. With his free hand, he jabbed the muzzle of his gun beneath the woman's chin.

"I've got this one," Eldon said. "Take care of the business over there." With that, Eldon peeked out from behind his cover and took a shot at Bryce.

The wounded gunman was still shambling toward Eldon, spitting out blood as he took another sloppy shot.

Clint wasn't about to waste time arguing with the bounty hunter, and turned to focus on Rob and the old woman.

"You'll be putting down that gun, Adams," Rob said. "And then granny and me are walking away."

"In case you haven't noticed, we're on a moving train,"

Clint said. "If you want to jump off, I'll hold the door for you." As he spoke, he soaked up every detail of the man he was facing. In an instant, he noted how Rob was standing, how he held his gun, how he held the old woman, even the tone of his voice.

"Back off, Adams." Rob's voice was steely, yet tense under all the pressure. "None of us want to see this here woman get hurt."

"You're a coward."

"What . . . did you . . . say?"

"I said you're a coward," Clint repeated. "Hiding behind a woman, holding the gun on her instead of me. Those are all things a coward does. You won't even look me in the eyes."

"Fuck you, Adams." Even as he said those words, lacing them with all the venom and defiance he could dredge up, Rob couldn't keep from sticking his head out from behind the old woman so he could look at Clint with both eyes.

When Clint looked into those eyes, he snapped his arm up just enough to aim directly between them, then pulled the trigger. The Colt bucked against his hand, spitting out his last bullet, which tunneled straight through Rob's skull.

As his head snapped back and his brains formed a weblike pattern on the window behind him, Rob tensed every one of his muscles with the reflex of death. His finger tightened around his trigger, but it wasn't enough to fire the gun. Instead, the barrel tapped against the old woman's jaw and then slipped from his fingers.

"You all right, ma'am?" Clint asked.

For a second, he thought she was going to scream. Her mouth opened and her eyes went wide, but no sound came out except for a rasping breath. Once the air was out of her, she swooned and started to drop.

Clint just managed to catch her.

• • •

"You . . ."

The word sounded more like a groan than any kind of language. It slipped from Bryce's mouth along with a spurt of blood as another of Eldon's bullets slammed into his body.

Bryce didn't seem to feel it, however. He was beyond pain. And in a matter of seconds, he was going to be beyond life itself.

"Yeah . . . you recognize me, don't you?" Eldon said with a grin. "I chased you down more than once for the things you done."

Lifting his arms with tremendous effort, Bryce pulled both his triggers and sent another wave of thunder through the air. One shot came close to its mark, but the other punched through the side of the car.

"Gonna . . . kill . . . you. . . ."

Eldon shook his head and stepped completely out from behind his cover. Standing in the aisle, he stared straight at the gunman and said, "Yeah. Sure you are."

With that, the inside of the passenger car erupted with a barrage of gunfire. Eldon fired first, sending a bullet that punched through Bryce's neck.

As his head snapped back and then lolled to one side, Bryce pulled one of his own triggers. The gunman's eyes were clearing up a little as the pain from the horrific wounds became too much to ignore. That improved his aim, however, and his last shot tore the flesh in Eldon's thigh.

Eldon staggered back, snarled a curse, and lowered his hand just a little bit, so that his next shot punched straight through Bryce's heart.

No matter how much hate was flowing through Bryce, it wasn't enough to overcome the fact that his blood was no longer moving through his veins. Once the bullet passed through his heart, all of the energy bled out of his body. No amount of adrenaline could maintain him any longer, and Bryce dropped to the floor as if lead weights had been attached to his back.

Eldon slid some fresh rounds into his gun and stepped over to look down at the fallen man. When he got close enough, he kicked the guns from Bryce's hands and snapped the cylinder of his own weapon shut with a flick of his wrist.

"You made a bad choice here, boy."

Bryce stared back at him with vacant eyes.

FORTY-TWO

Willa burst through the back door of the passenger car, her gun in her hand. She immediately crouched behind the rear set of benches and looked around for something to shoot at. All she could see was a bunch of petrified faces staring back at her.

"It's all right," Clint said from the front of the car. "Put your gun away. It's all over."

After holstering her .45, Willa walked cautiously down the aisle to where Clint and Eldon were standing. "What the hell was all that shooting about?" she asked.

Clint had just gotten the old woman to a seat and was moving to stand beside Eldon. "Where's the sheriff?"

"With James," she replied, pointing toward the other car. "We heard the shooting, and he barricaded himself back there. I'd be awful careful heading that way if I were you. Now how about answering my question. What was all of this about?"

Clint looked over to Eldon. "I was just about to ask Eldon here that same question."

"He recognized me," Eldon said, holstering his gun. "I'd gone after this one a while back after a train robbery.

The railroad was putting a big enough price on their heads and didn't care how they were brought in. I tracked these two for nearly two months straight and faced them down twice."

"So how come all of you were still alive to meet today?" Willa asked.

"I said I faced them down . . . not killed them. I got a few of their partners, but these two were awful slippery." Eldon looked down and tapped the toe of his boot against the side of Bryce's head. "I had this one at gunpoint and was about to finish him off one time. He swore he'd come after me and make me pay for that if he lived. I guess he was a man of his word."

Clint listened to Eldon's story and then looked at Willa. A look passed between them, and she was just about to say something when Clint subtly shook his head. She got the hint and kept her silence.

"What about Stohls or our prisoner?" Clint asked. "Do these two have any connection to them?"

"I managed to take a healthy gouge out of their old gang, so it stands to reason that they'd be ready to hook up with the likes of Stohls and James."

"Were they the type to break James out?"

Eldon nodded. "They've tried jailbreaks before, but got only one to work. It looks like they haven't been practicing too much."

"So were they at the robbery in Coverdale?" Clint asked. He looked at Eldon and Willa in turn, but didn't get a reply right away.

Before long, Willa shrugged. "To be honest, the deputies were saying that some of the gang might have escaped. I don't recall seeing their faces."

Looking up at Clint, Eldon shrugged, too. "They were no strangers to jobs like that one . . . but I didn't set eyes on them that night either. I was there with the deputies and Sheriff Grayson nearly from the start. There were killers all over that bank. Some were inside, some were out front, and there were more out back. The more I think about it, the more everything starts to blend together."

Clint tried to think, but the passengers were starting to poke their heads out into the open once again and their voices were filling the car. "See to these folks, Willa. Check if any of them are hurt. Start in the back and work your way toward us. We'll check the front and move back."

She didn't look happy about the assignment, but started doing it nonetheless. Glancing down at the cowering people, she began helping them to their feet and searching for any bleeders. Her manner was rough, but so was almost everything else about her.

Satisfied that she was doing her job well enough, Clint left Willa to it and turned back to face Eldon. "I saw that man's face," he said to the bounty hunter, pointing down at Bryce. "He started shooting the minute he laid eyes on you. They didn't do that when they saw me."

"What's the matter, Adams? Not used to being somewhere besides the center of the universe? Are you so damn important that everyone in their right mind should consider you the biggest dog in the yard?"

Clint didn't know exactly how to respond to that. None of Eldon's words were ringing true, and there was something missing in the equation that Clint just wasn't seeing. Not yet, anyway. And rather than try to piece everything together in the middle of a group of panicked civilians, he decided to let it drop for the moment and come back to it later. He was certain that, whatever it was, it would wait for him.

". . . Y . . . you. . . ."

The muttered voice came from somewhere down by

Clint's feet. When he saw who was talking, he could scarcely believe it.

Somehow . . . some way . . . Bryce Corday was clinging to a last thread of life. The gunman couldn't move anything but his eyelids and mouth. His skin was pale and bloody. He struggled to get out his last words.

Clint knelt down to Bryce's level when it looked like the killer was about to try and speak again.

It took nearly all of his strength, but Bryce managed to look beyond the man closest to him and glare at Eldon. ". . . You . . . you're . . ."

Clint tried to make out the rest of what Bryce was saying, but couldn't hear more than wet gurgles. The one thing that was for sure was that Bryce's words were directed toward Eldon. When Clint looked up at the bounty hunter, he saw that Eldon already had his gun out and was pointing it downward.

Clint threw himself to one side and plucked the Colt from his holster, but not before Eldon got a shot off that punched through the center of Bryce's forehead and put his lights out for good.

"He was going for a gun," Eldon said, lowering his pistol and dropping it into his holster.

Looking back toward the man on the floor, Clint saw that one of Bryce's hands was lying over his gunbelt and the other was on the ground. When Clint moved the hand over the gunbelt aside, he saw that the holster was empty.

Eldon shrugged as Clint stood up. "Honest mistake."

FORTY-THREE

Panic simmered like water on a stove until the engineer pulled up to their first scheduled stop. The passengers settled for a bit, but didn't truly regain their senses until they had the opportunity to get off the train and stretch their legs on the platform.

Some of them were scheduled to get off there, and were more than happy to see the shabby little station. Some just needed to get some fresh air while local deputies cleared out the bodies of Rob Emmerson and Bryce Corday. Others left the platform so fast that they forgot about their bags. Their tickets were for Raleigh, but they just wanted to put the train behind them.

Clint and Willa posted themselves outside and patrolled the platform, keeping their eyes out for anyone suspicious trying to board the train. They also were looking for familiar faces among the crowd. One local deputy went with each of them to lend their eyes to the effort.

The passengers boarded, and the train was away from the station in record time. Clint didn't feel the first bit of relief until the scenery was speeding by them. Even then, he and Willa kept close to the sheriff.

Watching James had become more than a favor to Mark. It was now a dangerous responsibility, and Clint wasn't going to rest until they'd delivered the bandit to the Raleigh jailhouse. More than that, he wasn't about to let the matter about Rob and Bryce drop solely on the basis of Eldon's explanation.

There was still a piece of the picture missing. Until he found out what it was, Clint was going to be ready for anything.

It had been a couple of hours since the train had gotten up to full speed again. The sun was low in the sky and the locomotive was speeding toward its destination. Everything was as quiet as it could be, considering that there was nearly a full load of passengers and Clint had made it his business to keep the rear of the second passenger car clear.

Having finished patrolling the sleeper car, Clint stepped through the doors connecting it to the passenger car. Willa was right where he'd left her, sitting on the last bench and keeping an eye on everyone in it.

Clint dropped onto the seat beside her and stretched out his legs. "How are you holding up?" he asked.

"Fine." Despite her simple response, it was plain to see that she was anything but fine. Her eyes never stopped moving. They darted like a nervous bird's as she glanced at every person inside the car, one at a time. When she'd made a complete cycle, she'd take a breath and start again.

Clint reached out and placed a finger beneath her chin so he could turn her head until she was looking directly at him. "Are you sure about that?"

She tried to keep up her facade, but let it drop after a few seconds. When she finally stopped staring at the rest of the car, her entire body seemed to relax. "I should have spotted those two. If I had, things might have turned out better. They might have—"

"Things turned out just fine," Clint interrupted. "Nobody else got hurt and those two killers didn't get what they came for."

"But that's what's been bothering me. I want to know what they were doing here."

"You don't think they were here to break out James?" Clint asked.

She smiled ever so slightly, shaking her head. "Not entirely. And neither do you, so just stop acting like everything's perfect and under control."

"You know something, don't you? Something you're not telling me."

After looking down for a moment, she looked back up and then nodded.

"I could tell," Clint said. "Ever since what happened with Eldon and those two in the other car. You looked like you had something to say, but just didn't know quite how to say it." He leaned a little closer, easing his hand around her shoulders. "It's just me now, Willa. Say what you want to, because there's nobody else around to hear you."

She looked around the car once more. This time, however, she moved her eyes a bit slower as they went from face to face. There weren't many passengers in the car with them, just the ones who'd been pushed out of the other one and hadn't heard enough about the prisoner transfer to be scared off.

As Willa glanced from face to face, she saw that none of the passengers were looking at her or Clint. Most of them were asleep, reading, or wrapped up in their own conversations. Those voices, combined with the clatter of wheels upon rails, were enough to drown out most normal speaking voices. Even so, when she spoke to him, she lowered her voice to just above a whisper.

"I've seen those two," she said.

"You mean the two who were shot in there?" Clint asked, nodding in the direction of the first passenger car.

Willa nodded. "They're . . . they were thieves and hired out their guns, but I only saw them with any of Stohls's men one other time. One of them had a cousin . . . some kid, named Tommy Corday, who figured himself as a bad man.

"Bryce . . . the one Eldon killed . . . he was Tommy's cousin, and he never did like that that kid wanted to get into any business other than shopkeeping or bookmaking. He kept Tommy away from Stohls and his men. He even killed someone over the matter."

"How do you know all of this?" Clint asked.

"It's my business to keep my ear to the ground whe. it comes to those types. No bounty hunter gets very far by relying on luck. Especially when you're in a business where most others think you don't belong. I've stayed alive and in the game this long because I know what the bad types are up to.

"Men talk to a pretty face and don't take any notice when I'm around. It used to get me riled up, but I found I could sure use it. I keep track of what's going on with killers and thieves, especially when they start biting at each other. After all," she said with a familiar smirk, "that's when it's even easier for me to pick them off. And when you see tension around a man like Stohls . . . with the money that's offered for him . . . you'd be wise to pay attention."

Clint wasn't the biggest admirer of bounty hunters, but he had to admit that Willa Singer was more than just a bounty hunter. At the very least, she was someone good at her job and an expert in her field. She figured the angles and played them well. As a man who knew the value of cunning and quick thinking, Clint admired those traits in her, especially since she'd been putting them to such good use.

"So there's really no way those two were here to break out James," Clint stated.

"No. There's no way in hell."

"Then maybe they were after Eldon. What have you heard about him?"

Willa looked over her shoulder, leaned closer, and lowered her voice a bit more. "That's just the thing. Members of my profession don't exactly get along. We try to keep our heads down as much as possible, but we still hear about one another from time to time."

"Yeah. So what have you heard about Eldon?"

"Not a damn thing. It's like he was put on this earth the night he tipped Sheriff Grayson about that robbery."

Clint didn't like the sound of that. Not one bit.

FORTY-FOUR

Mark sat in the middle compartment of the sleeper car, on the same stool that he'd been warming since the train pulled out of Coverdale. He'd started out thinking that he should be the one watching the prisoner because he was the only real lawman of the bunch. The reason for that was because he'd figured the transfer would be a cakewalk.

There was only one man in chains; the rest of his gang was dead. And if James decided to start any trouble, Mark still had one hell of an ace up his sleeve by the name of Clint Adams. Nobody could have asked for better backup than The Gunsmith himself. But still, more men were dead, and Mark was cursing himself for taking this job so lightly.

With Stohls dead, any stragglers from the gang had no reason to stay around. The job had been a failure, and bounty hunters were claiming bodies to be shipped off for reward. Mark had even thought about going to the mail car so he could look inside the pine box Eldon had dragged aboard, just to satisfy himself that Stohls was dead.

Behind him, the door opened and Eldon stepped inside.

"Got a minute, Sheriff?" the bounty hunter asked.

"No."

"Mister Adams wants to talk to you. By the looks of him, I'd say it was something pretty important."

Mark let out a heavy sigh and stood up. "What's so important that he can't come in here?"

"Oh, go on," Eldon said. "You need to stretch your legs and get something to eat before you keel over. I'll watch this one here." When he saw the uncomfortable look on the sheriff's face, Eldon added, "Send that gal back here as well, then. We'll watch ol' James for ya. We've got to make sure he's still breathin' when we roll into Raleigh. He's worth a lot more to us that way."

In a strange way, the sheriff took some comfort from the bounty hunters' mercenary attitude. Nodding, he said, "All right. But if he so much as moves . . . make him sorry."

"Sure thing, Sheriff," Eldon said, removing his pistol from its holster. "I'm real good at knowing which pieces I can cut without doing any permanent damage."

Mark nodded and turned to walk out. His hand was on the door handle when there was a sharp, blinding pain at the back of his head. He thought his skull had suddenly cracked open, and as that sensation washed through him, he felt himself start to fall over. He blacked out before he hit the floor.

"What the hell took you so long?" James asked. He was sitting on the edge of the room's narrow bed with his arms strung through the thick wooden headboard. Willa's handcuffs had been traded for a set provided by the sheriff.

Eldon stood over the sheriff with the gun in his hand. The butt was dripping blood from when it had smashed into the back of Mark's skull. Grabbing hold of the law-

man's shirt, he pulled him away from the door and propped him up against the wall.

"Sorry about that, but we both knew we had to make some sacrifices if this was going to work."

"Yeah, but I see your sacrifices didn't involve spending your nights chained up like a dog."

"No, but kissing the law's ass was worse."

"How'd you get so close, anyway?"

Eldon smiled as he went through Mark's pockets. "You'd be amazed at what a clean shave can do for a man. I cut myself up pretty good because I was in such a rush, but I managed well enough."

"It doesn't hurt that your picture on all those posters made you look so good."

"Yeah, well, they were pretty old. Besides, most folks didn't want to admit they'd been taken out by someone who wasn't a tough young pup full of piss and vinegar. Either way . . . it all worked out, didn't it?"

"Yeah, Kevin. It sure did."

Without the beard covering the bottom half of his face, Kevin Stohls looked both thinner and older. The narrow shape of his face could be seen better, along with the flecks of gray that had worked their way into his eyebrows and hairline. That gray had been there before, but it had been eclipsed by the dark bush growing from his chin and beneath his nose.

Stohls held up the small key that he'd found in one of Mark's inner pockets. The key fit perfectly into James's cuffs, and with a twist, the manacles were open.

Rubbing his wrists and straightening his back after what felt like a year, James asked, "What are we going to do about those others?"

"We kill them, and then a few of the passengers as well. I scoped out a few in the next car who look perfect. All we need to do is blast them in the face the way I did

Tommy, and no one will know it's not us. The passengers are too scared to do anything if they hear a scuffle, and when they do screw up the guts to look back here, they'll see everyone dead."

"And you figure they'll think we all killed each other?"

"They're sheep," Stohls said. "They'll believe whatever's easiest to believe. All we need to do is feed them the story we want, and they'll swallow it down."

James nodded and smiled for the first time in days. "Every once in a while, I'm glad I didn't kill you when I had the chance."

Stohls grinned and pulled a holdout pistol from his boot. "No matter how highly you think of yourself, you never had a chance like that."

"Yeah, yeah. What about him?" James said, nodding toward the crumpled figure of the sheriff.

"We'll finish him off once we get the others. It wouldn't do to make any more noise than we have to. Now get your hands back down there and look like you did before."

Stohls waited until his partner was back down on the bed with his hands laced through the boards and his gun hidden beneath his left elbow. Then he took a breath and let his face fall back into the expression he'd worn as Eldon Masters.

Sticking his head into the hall, Stohls said, "Hey, you two. Come back here for a moment, would ya?"

FORTY-FIVE

"What was that?" Clint stood up from his bench and looked toward the back of the car and the door leading to the sleeper. "Did you hear that, too?"

Willa nodded once. "Yeah. It sounded like something fell."

Clint moved toward the door and pressed an ear to the wood. All he could hear was the rattle of the train and the rush of air outside. He eased open the door and stepped onto the small platform spanning the two cars. Just then, he heard Eldon's voice coming from the sleeper.

Standing directly behind him, Willa touched Clint's shoulder to let him know she was there. Clint motioned for her to move onto the platform, then reached for the next door and pulled it open.

Eldon was still looking out into the hall. The expression on his face was surprised. "There you are. Come on over here for a second."

Willa pushed past Clint and stormed into the sleeper car. "I want to speak to the sheriff."

"Sure. He's right in here and wants to have a word with you, too."

Clint followed her and shut the door. There was something odd about the look in Eldon's eyes. And there was something imposing that hadn't been there before. He was going to tell Willa to hold back for a second when a shot erupted from the room where the prisoner was being held.

Clint's first reaction was to charge in there, but he managed to hold back for a second and then lunge forward, keeping low to the floor. He heard something drop and saw Willa's hair spill out of the room where her head must have hit the floor. Another shot blazed through the air, tearing over Clint's head in the spot where his heart would have been if he'd followed his first instinct.

When Clint could finally look inside the room, he saw Eldon standing there with a smoking gun in hand. Willa lying on the floor, not far from the sheriff.

Stohls looked down at Clint with his intentions written all over his face. Knowing he was too vulnerable where he was, Clint threw himself to one side and rolled out of the doorway.

"I see where *his* loyalties are," Stohls said. Turning to Willa, he saw that she was already going for her gun. "Now that's what I call spirit," he said. "Normally, I like that in a woman. Not today, though."

Stohls was about to fire when he saw a flicker of motion from the corner of his eye. Without the slightest hesitation, he swiveled toward the doorway and tightened his grip on his trigger. He might have put a bullet into Clint's chest if it hadn't been for a hand reaching up from the floor and pulling him off balance.

"No," Mark grunted as he pulled on Stohls's leg.

Stohls kicked free of the sheriff's grip and heard a voice coming from behind him.

"That's far enough," Clint said, pointing the gun at Stohls. "Now we see where *your* loyalties lie. Why are you doing this?"

Shaking his head, Stohls just knew that Clint Adams was more ready to talk than to shoot. He didn't say a word to The Gunsmith as he raised his gun to take his shot. Before he could get the barrel pointing at Clint, a shot roared through the room and lifted Stohls off his feet.

Clint tilted his head and shrugged. He hadn't even had to fire. "Glad you still had that in you," he said to Willa.

Lying on the floor, she clasped her hand to her stomach and lowered the gun she'd used to kill Stohls. "Me, too. Now how about you help me up before I bleed to death."

Before lending his hand to the wounded pair on the floor, Clint looked over to James. He thought the prisoner looked a little too calm. Also, there was something missing . . . a glint of metal around his wrists.

Sensing that he'd been spotted, James rolled back against the wall and pulled his hands out from where he'd been holding them. The gun Stohls had given him was right where he'd left it, and all he had to do was grab it and pull the trigger.

James moved with the speed of the desperate. He knew everything was riding on that one shot, and every bit of experience he'd gotten over years of gunfighting came to play. In the blink of an eye, James had the gun in his hand, aimed it, and was tensing his finger on the trigger.

So far . . . Clint had yet to move a muscle.

With the hammer on James's gun a hair's breadth from dropping, Clint snapped his arm upward and pointed the Colt as though he was simply pointing his finger. The modified pistol, every bit as much a part of him as the hand that fired it, barked once, sending a bullet into James's chest.

The prisoner's body slammed against the wall as his heart exploded inside of him. His sudden movement caused his arm to twitch, which sent his shot into the wall next to Clint's head.

"Are . . . are there any more of them?" Mark grunted.

"I don't know, but we're taking these two to Raleigh. We came too far to leave this job unfinished. If there's another welcoming committee like this one, I'm sure they'll head for the hills once they hear about what's happened. In the meantime, we need to get you two to a doctor."

The deputies waiting for the train knew Stohls on sight, beard or not. Apparently that was why the gang hadn't been near North Carolina for some time. The lawmen were even more happy to see the outlaws returning to their city feet first. Clint looked over to the two gunmen as they were being taken away. Suddenly, a memory slipped into his head. Even all those miles away from that parlor, Clint couldn't help but remember the portly undertaker who would have been more than happy to sink his fingers into their remains.

"I'll say hello to the undertaker for you," he said, nodding once to the corpses.

Watch for

WIDOW'S WATCH

257th novel in the exciting GUNSMITH series
from Jove

Coming in May!